HOME

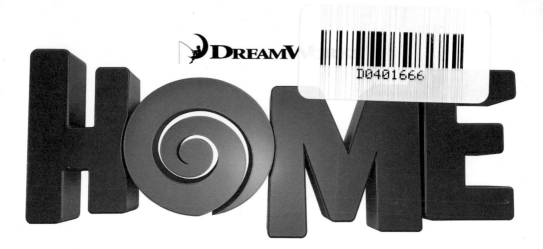

Volume One: Hide & Seek & Oh

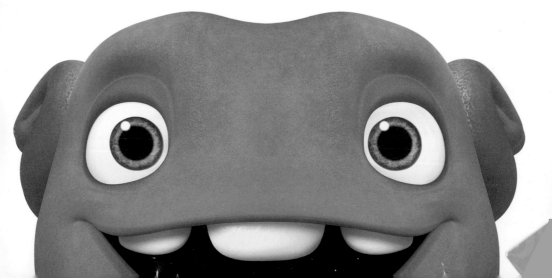

DreamWorks

HOME

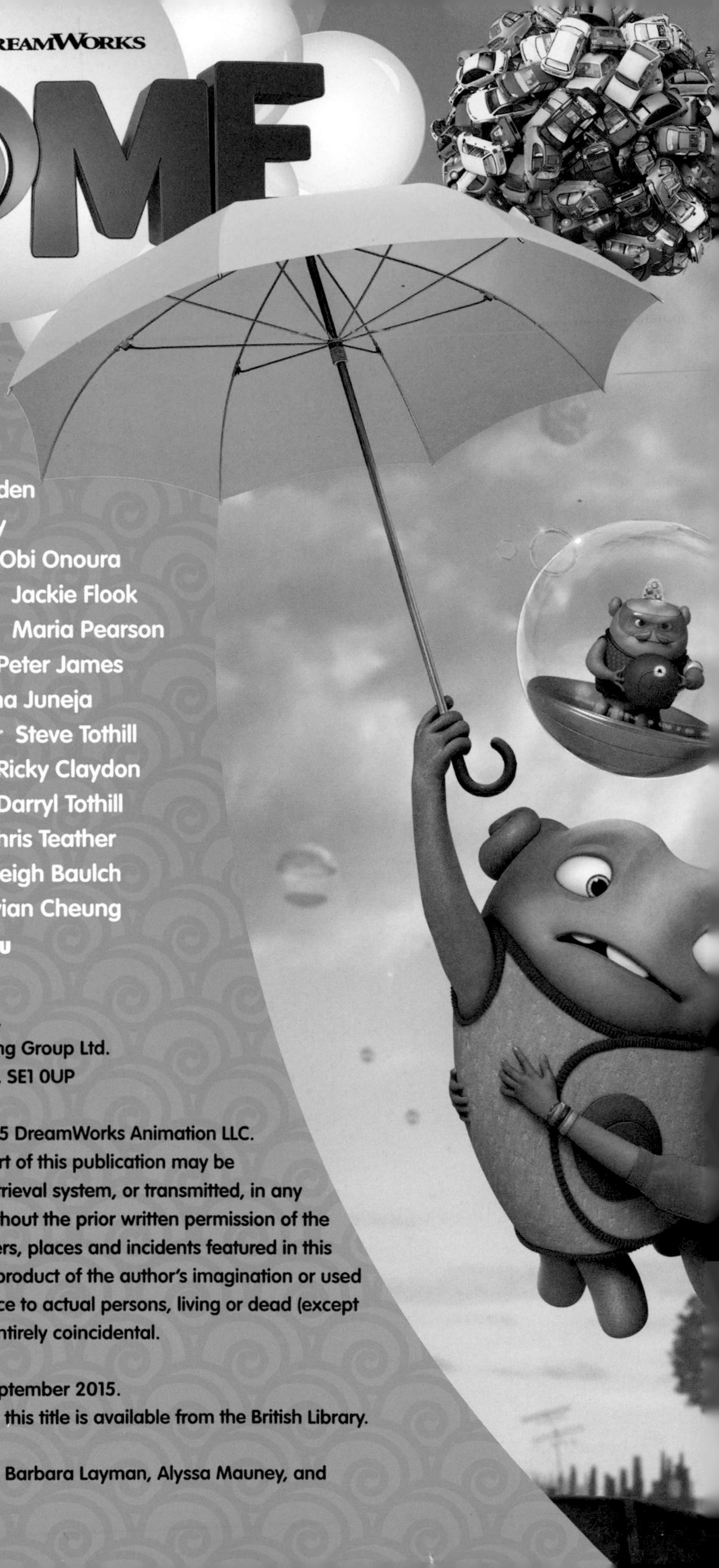

TITAN COMICS
Senior Editor Martin Eden
Designer Claire Geary
Production Manager Obi Onoura
Production Supervisor Jackie Flook
Production Supervisor Maria Pearson
Production Assistant Peter James
Studio Manager Selina Juneja
Senior Sales Manager Steve Tothill
Marketing Manager Ricky Claydon
Publishing Manager Darryl Tothill
Publishing Director Chris Teather
Operations Director Leigh Baulch
Executive Director Vivian Cheung
Publisher Nick Landau

ISBN: 9781782762287
Published by Titan Comics,
a division of Titan Publishing Group Ltd.
144 Southwark St. London, SE1 0UP

10 9 8 7 6 5 4 3 2 1
First printed in China in September 2015.
A CIP catalogue record for this title is available from the British Library.
Titan Comics. TC0532
Thanks to Corinne Combs, Barbara Layman, Alyssa Mauney, and Lawrence Hamashima.

INSIDE:

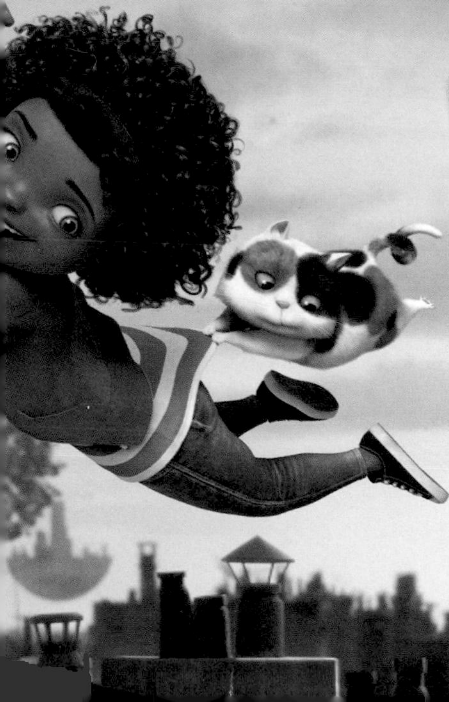

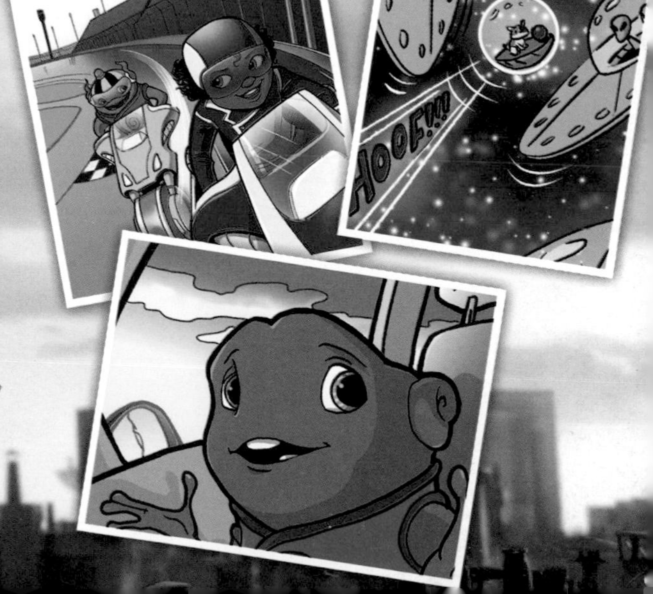

HOOF!!!

MEET THE

THE BOOV

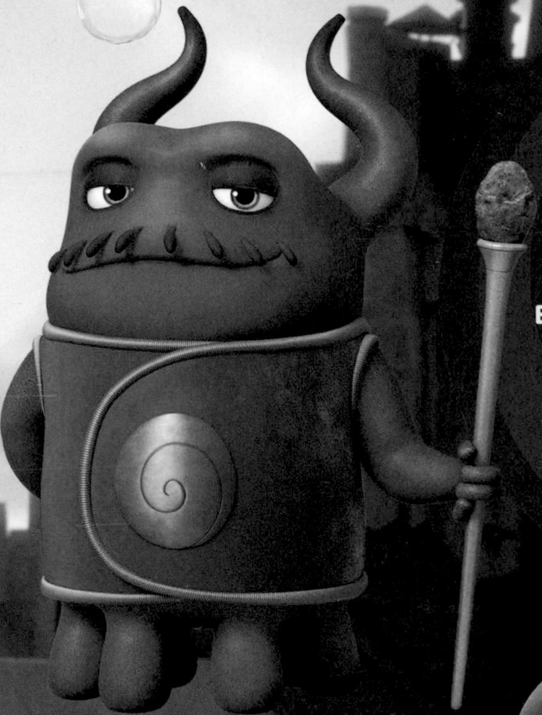

A gentle and cowardly alien race, the Boov motto is: 'It is never too late to run away!' Led by supreme leader Captain Smek, the Boov arrive on planet Earth to colonize it through a friendly invasion… but Earth isn't how it appeared in the pamphlet...!

Most Likely To: Invade your planet; Run away from danger

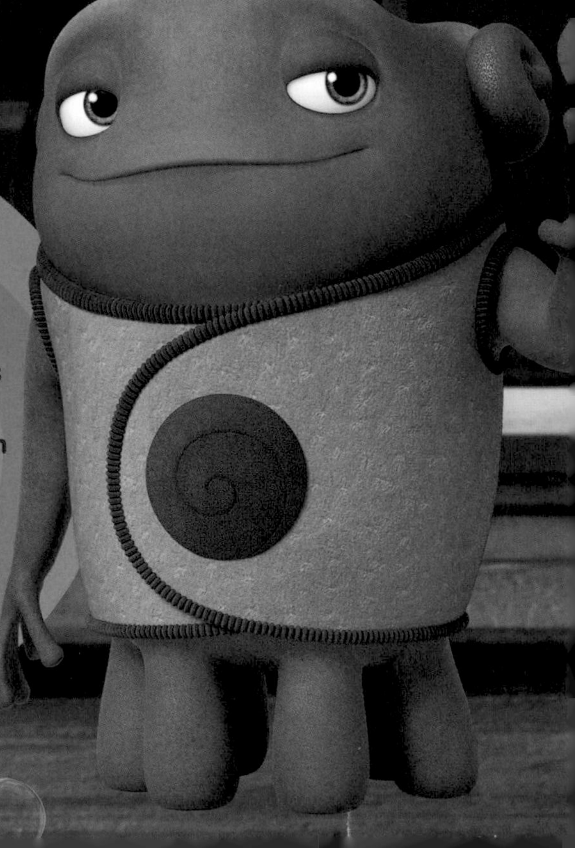

OH

Friendly and excitable, this Boov is unlike the rest of his species! Oh has lots to learn about social skills, but he's great with technology… he even turns Tip's car into a hovercar that runs on slushy drinks!

Most Likely To: Befriend you; Make a mistake; Overheat his core while dancing

HOME CREW!

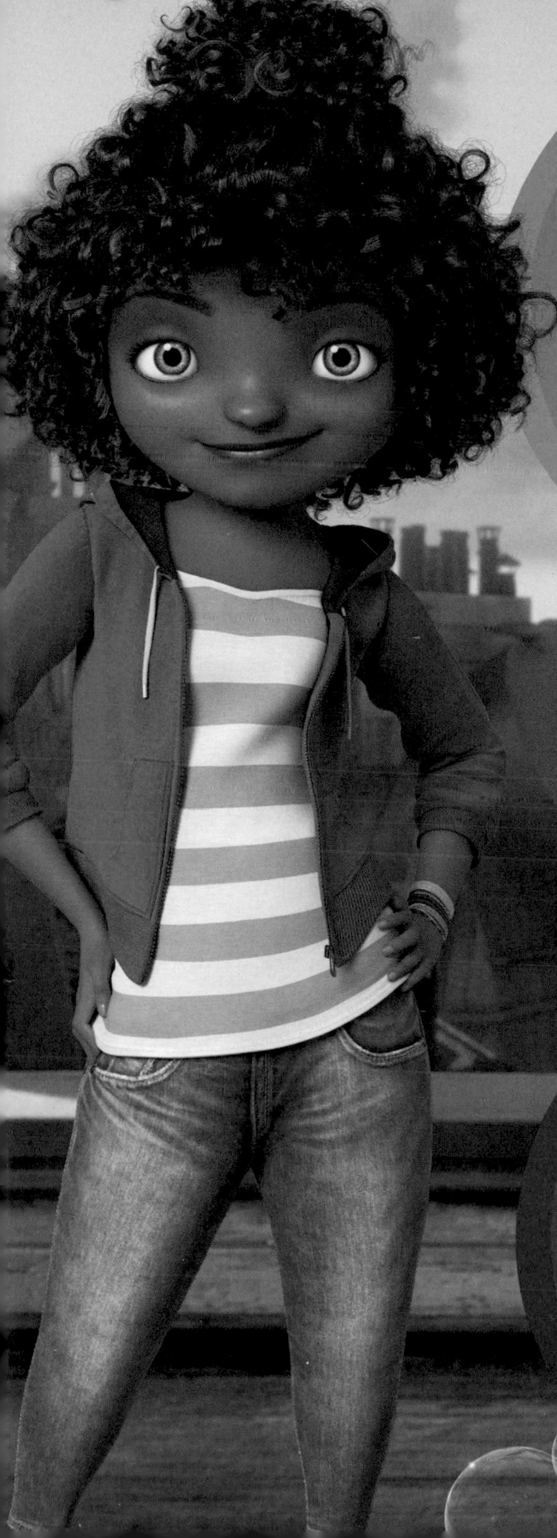

TIP

Tough and smart, Gratuity 'Tip' Tucci has a spirit of adventure. Tip moved to America from Barbados and found it hard to fit in at school, but she has fun with her little cat, Pig. When Tip meets Oh, it is the start of true friendship, misunderstood jokes… and chaos!

Most Likely To: Tell you a joke; Give a Boov a makeover; Run towards danger

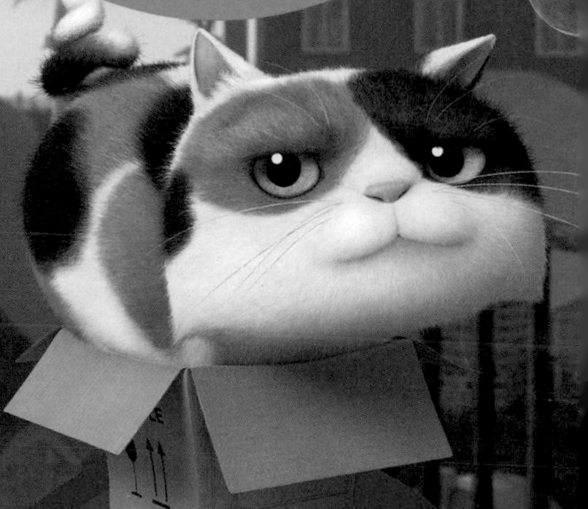

PIG

Arguably the cutest animal sidekick in the universe, Pig the cat is often found curled up on Tip, freaking Oh out with loud purring, or causing some kind of adorable mischief.

Most Likely To: Sit on Oh's head

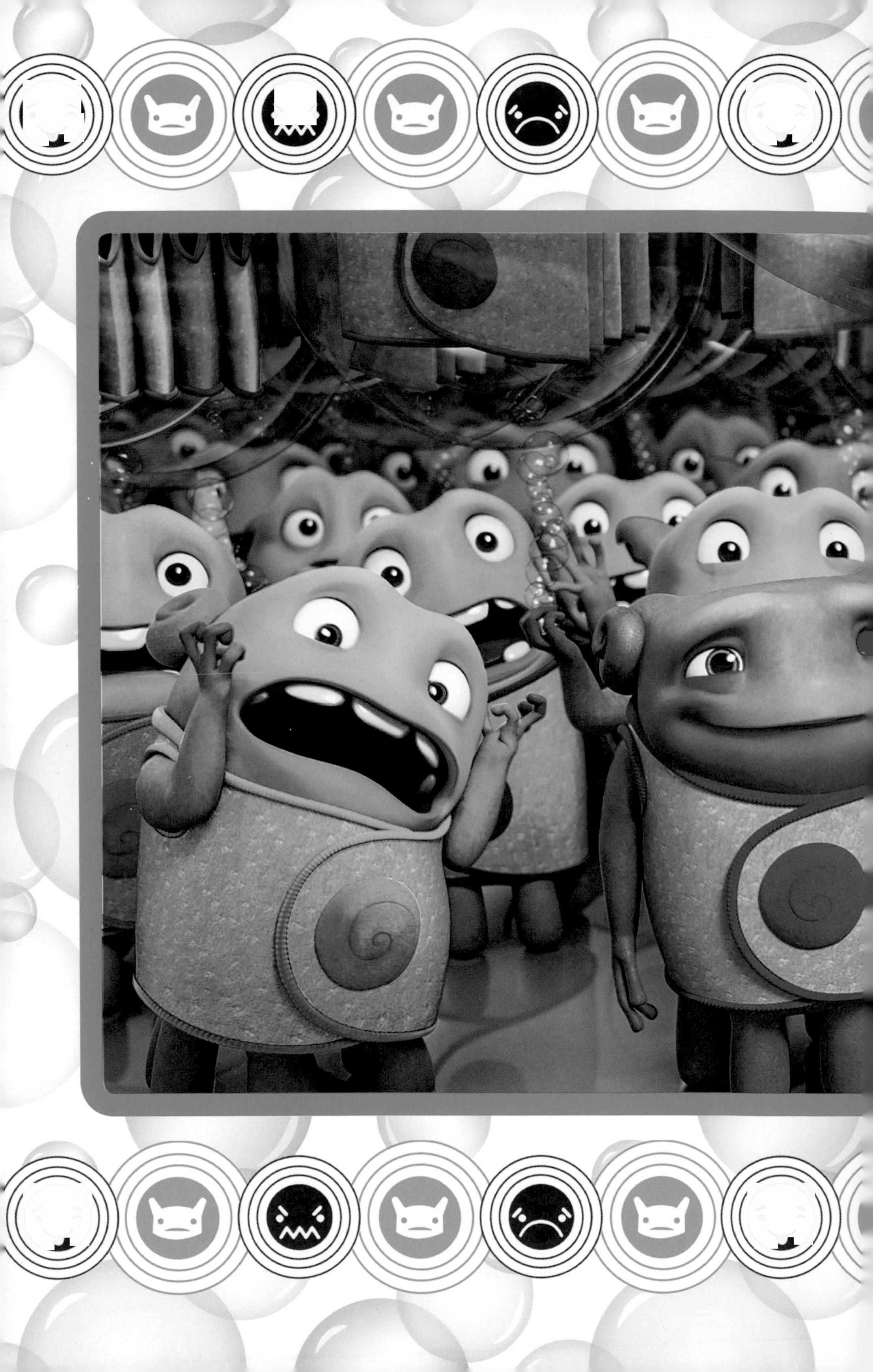

HIDE & SEEK & OH

WRITER Max Davison
PENCILS Matt Hebb
INKS Jason Worthington
COLORS Tracy Bailey
LETTERS Jim Campbell

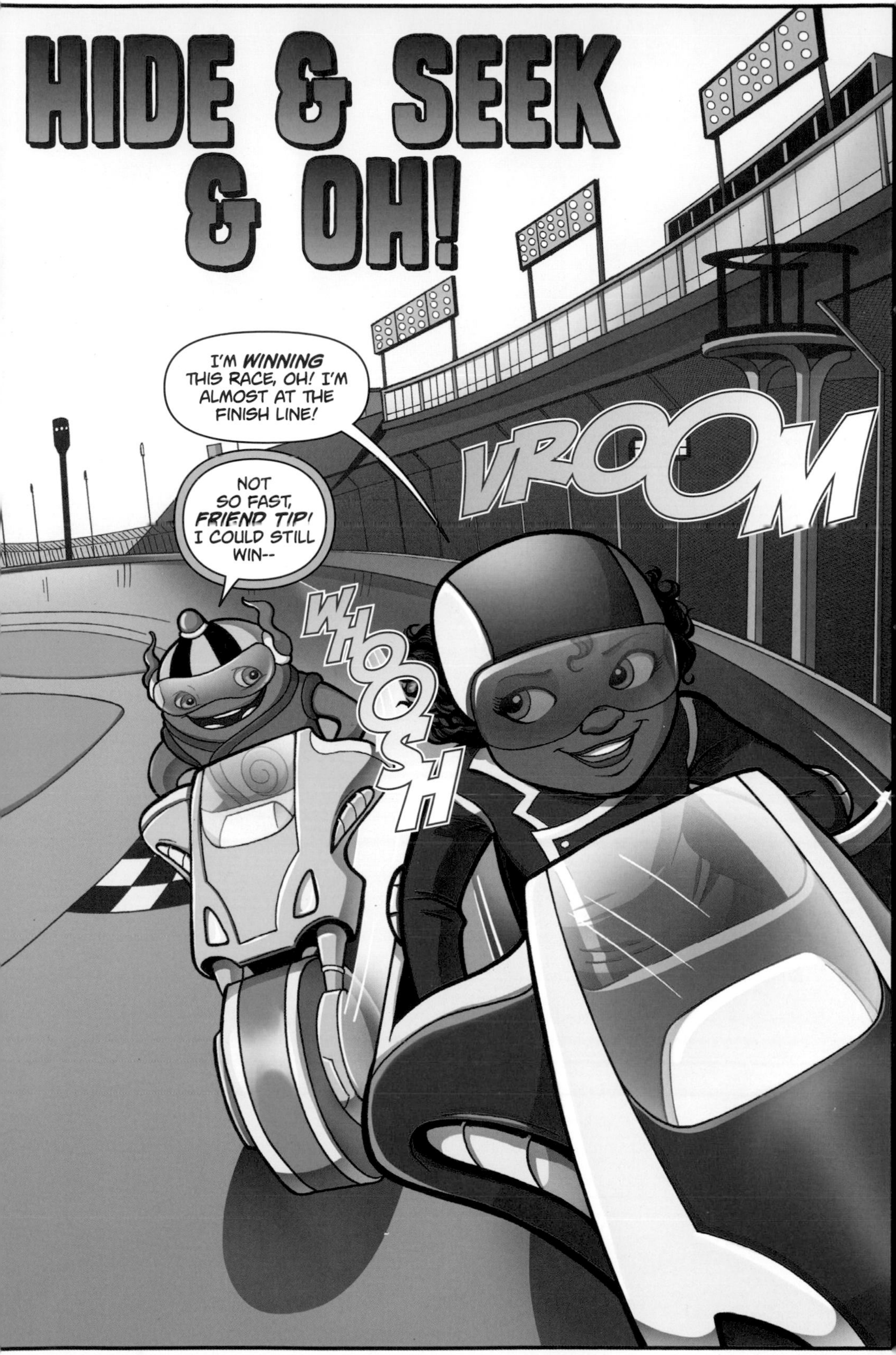
HIDE & SEEK & OH!
I'M *WINNING* THIS RACE, OH! I'M ALMOST AT THE FINISH LINE!
NOT SO FAST, *FRIEND TIP!* I COULD STILL WIN--
VROOM
WHOOSH

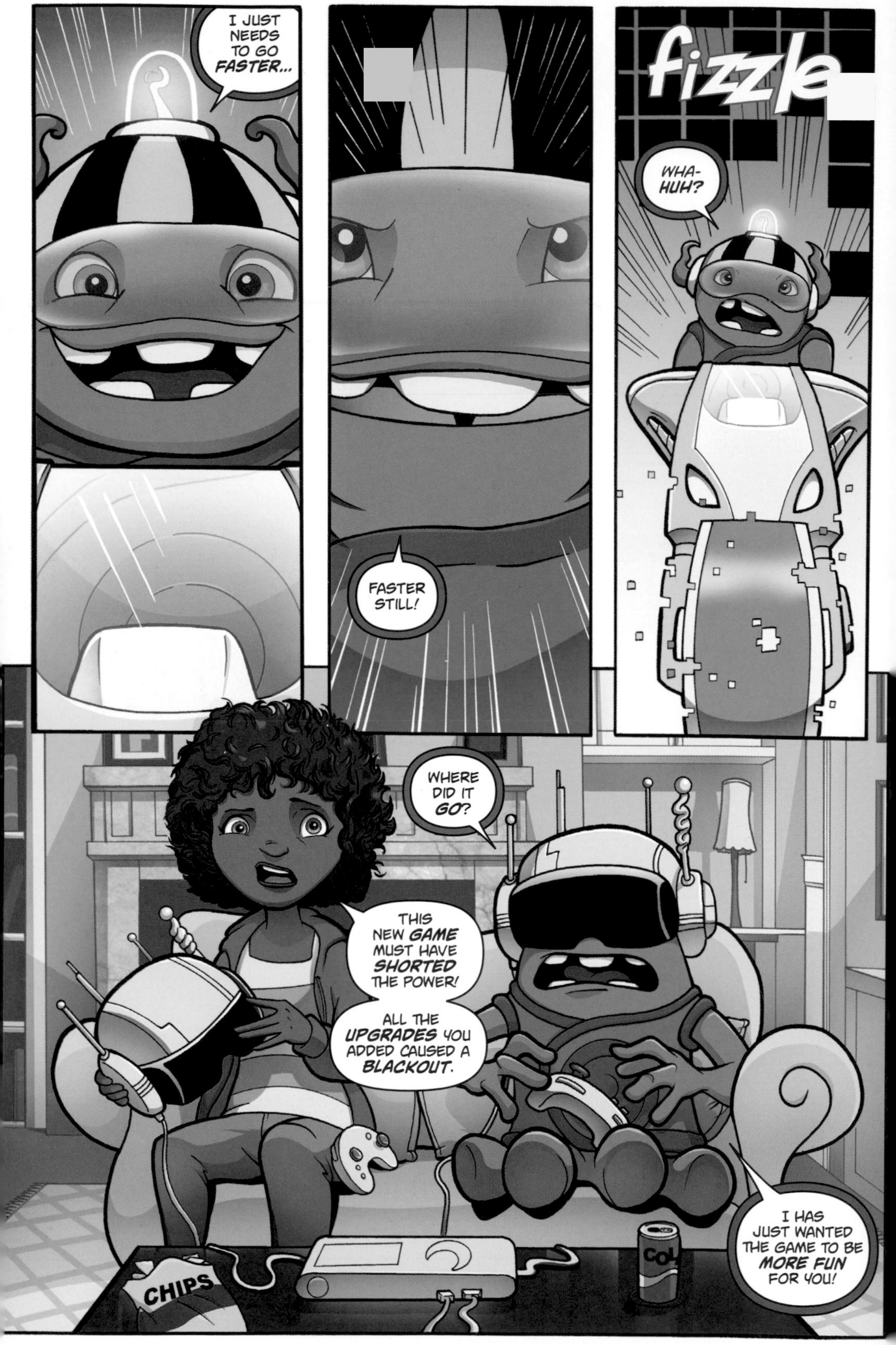
I JUST NEEDS TO GO FASTER...
FASTER STILL!
fizzle
WHA-HUH?
WHERE DID IT GO?
THIS NEW GAME MUST HAVE SHORTED THE POWER!
ALL THE UPGRADES YOU ADDED CAUSED A BLACKOUT.
I HAS JUST WANTED THE GAME TO BE MORE FUN FOR YOU!
CHIPS
COL

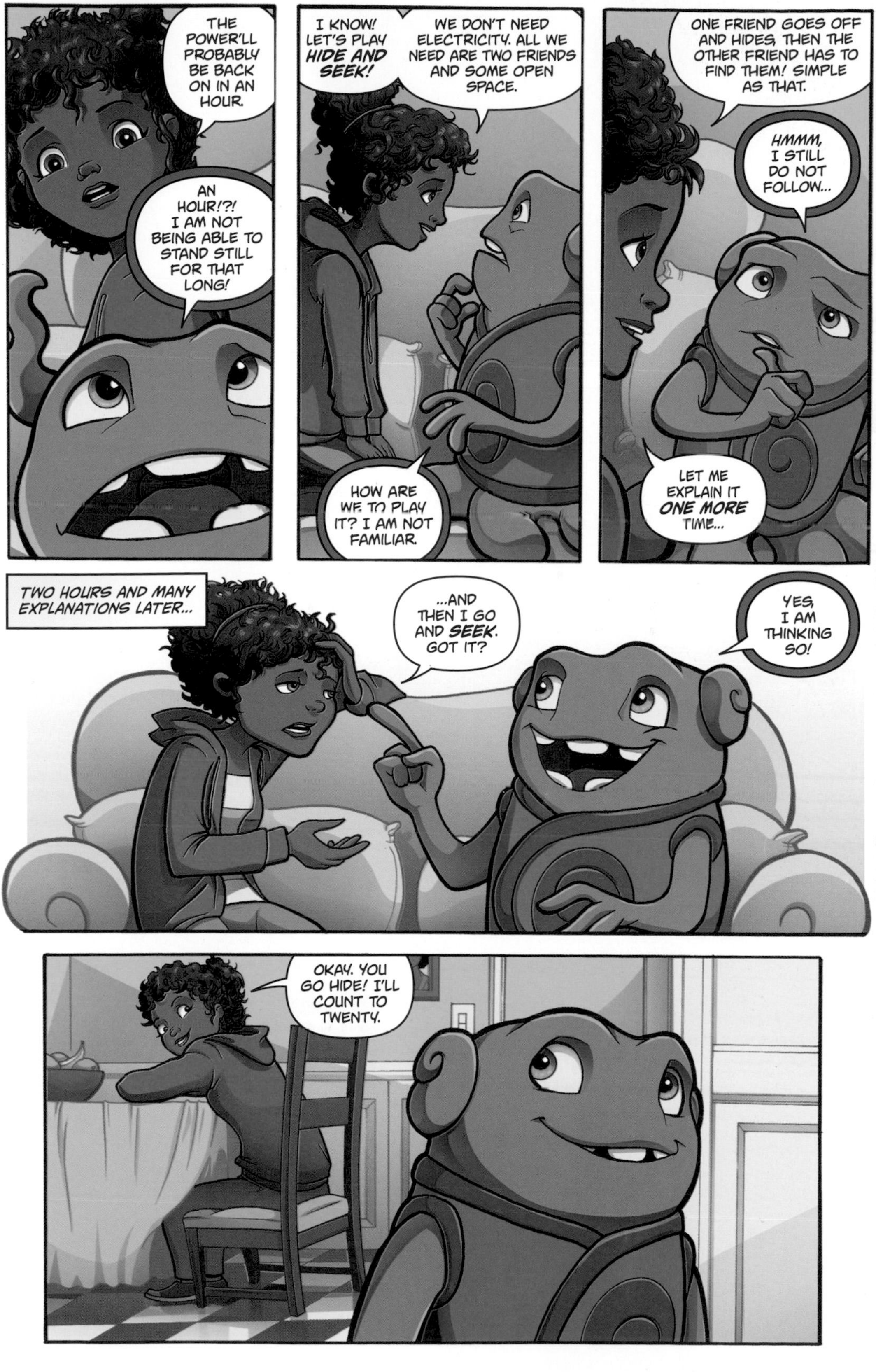
THE POWER'LL PROBABLY BE BACK ON IN AN HOUR.
AN HOUR!?! I AM NOT BEING ABLE TO STAND STILL FOR THAT LONG!
I KNOW! LET'S PLAY HIDE AND SEEK!
WE DON'T NEED ELECTRICITY. ALL WE NEED ARE TWO FRIENDS AND SOME OPEN SPACE.
HOW ARE WE TO PLAY IT? I AM NOT FAMILIAR.
ONE FRIEND GOES OFF AND HIDES, THEN THE OTHER FRIEND HAS TO FIND THEM! SIMPLE AS THAT.
HMMM, I STILL DO NOT FOLLOW...
LET ME EXPLAIN IT ONE MORE TIME...
TWO HOURS AND MANY EXPLANATIONS LATER...
...AND THEN I GO AND SEEK. GOT IT?
YES, I AM THINKING SO!
OKAY. YOU GO HIDE! I'LL COUNT TO TWENTY.

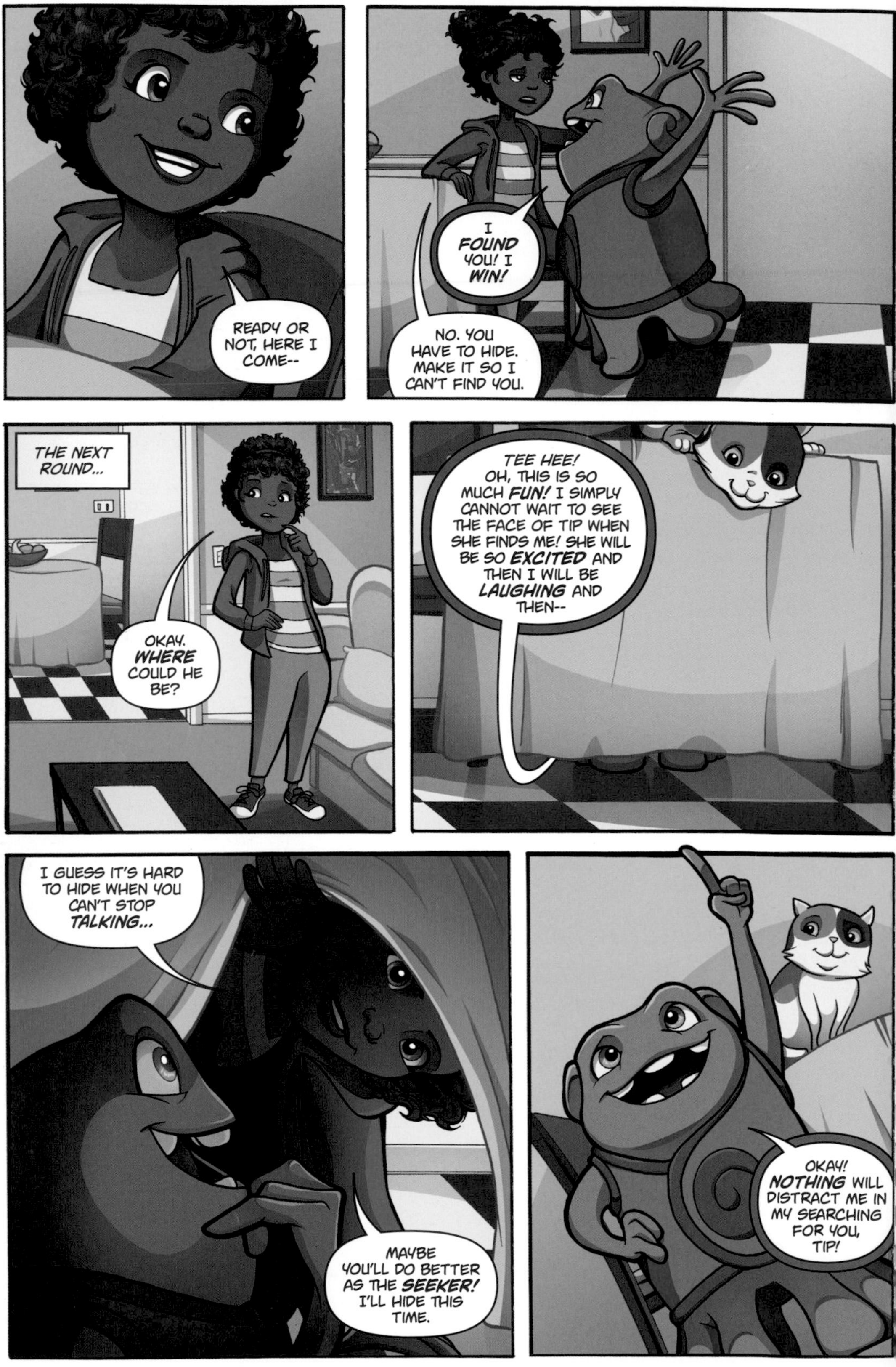
READY OR NOT, HERE I COME--
I FOUND YOU! I WIN!
NO. YOU HAVE TO HIDE. MAKE IT SO I CAN'T FIND YOU.
THE NEXT ROUND...
OKAY. WHERE COULD HE BE?
TEE HEE! OH, THIS IS SO MUCH FUN! I SIMPLY CANNOT WAIT TO SEE THE FACE OF TIP WHEN SHE FINDS ME! SHE WILL BE SO EXCITED AND THEN I WILL BE LAUGHING AND THEN--
I GUESS IT'S HARD TO HIDE WHEN YOU CAN'T STOP TALKING...
MAYBE YOU'LL DO BETTER AS THE SEEKER! I'LL HIDE THIS TIME.
OKAY! NOTHING WILL DISTRACT ME IN MY SEARCHING FOR YOU, TIP!

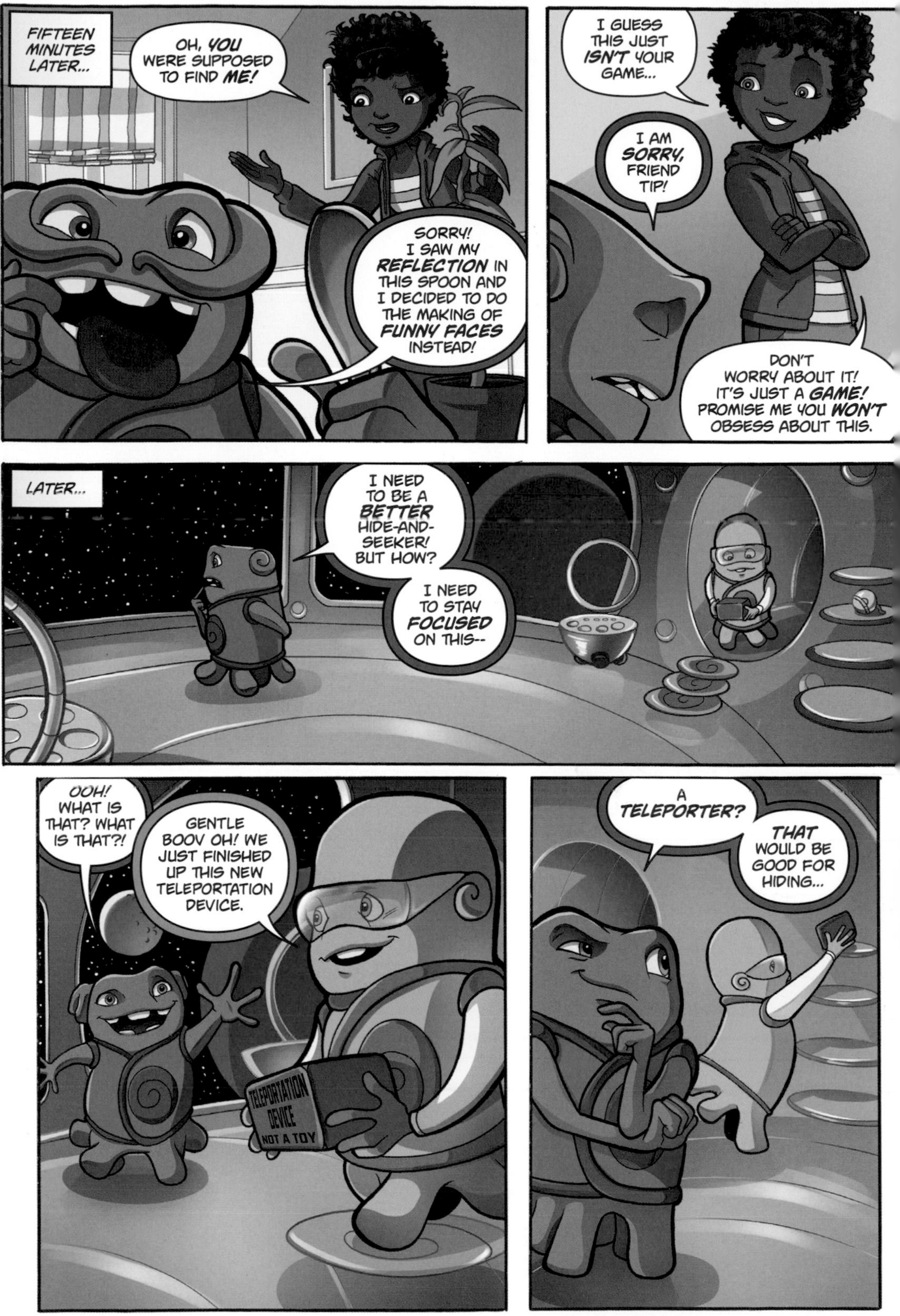
FIFTEEN MINUTES LATER...
OH, YOU WERE SUPPOSED TO FIND ME!
SORRY! I SAW MY REFLECTION IN THIS SPOON AND I DECIDED TO DO THE MAKING OF FUNNY FACES INSTEAD!
I GUESS THIS JUST ISN'T YOUR GAME...
I AM SORRY, FRIEND TIP!
DON'T WORRY ABOUT IT! IT'S JUST A GAME! PROMISE ME YOU WON'T OBSESS ABOUT THIS.
LATER...
I NEED TO BE A BETTER HIDE-AND-SEEKER! BUT HOW?
I NEED TO STAY FOCUSED ON THIS--
OOH! WHAT IS THAT? WHAT IS THAT?!
GENTLE BOOV OH! WE JUST FINISHED UP THIS NEW TELEPORTATION DEVICE.
TELEPORTATION DEVICE
NOT A TOY
A TELEPORTER?
THAT WOULD BE GOOD FOR HIDING...

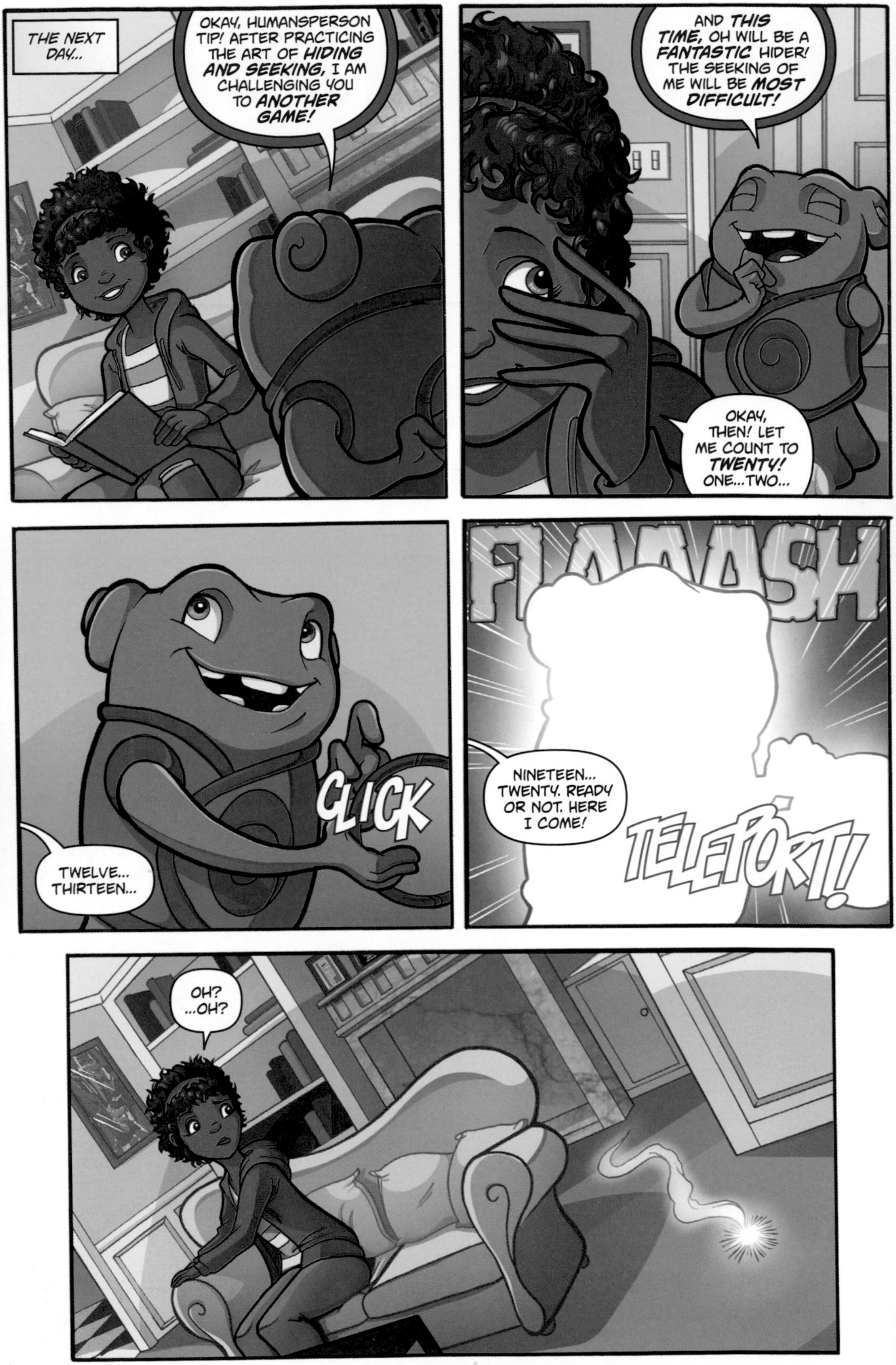
THE NEXT DAY...
OKAY, HUMANSPERSON TIP! AFTER PRACTICING THE ART OF HIDING AND SEEKING, I AM CHALLENGING YOU TO ANOTHER GAME!
AND THIS TIME, OH WILL BE A FANTASTIC HIDER! THE SEEKING OF ME WILL BE MOST DIFFICULT!
OKAY, THEN! LET ME COUNT TO TWENTY! ONE...TWO...
CLICK
TWELVE... THIRTEEN...
FLAAASH
NINETEEN... TWENTY. READY OR NOT. HERE I COME!
TELEPORT!
OH? ...OH?

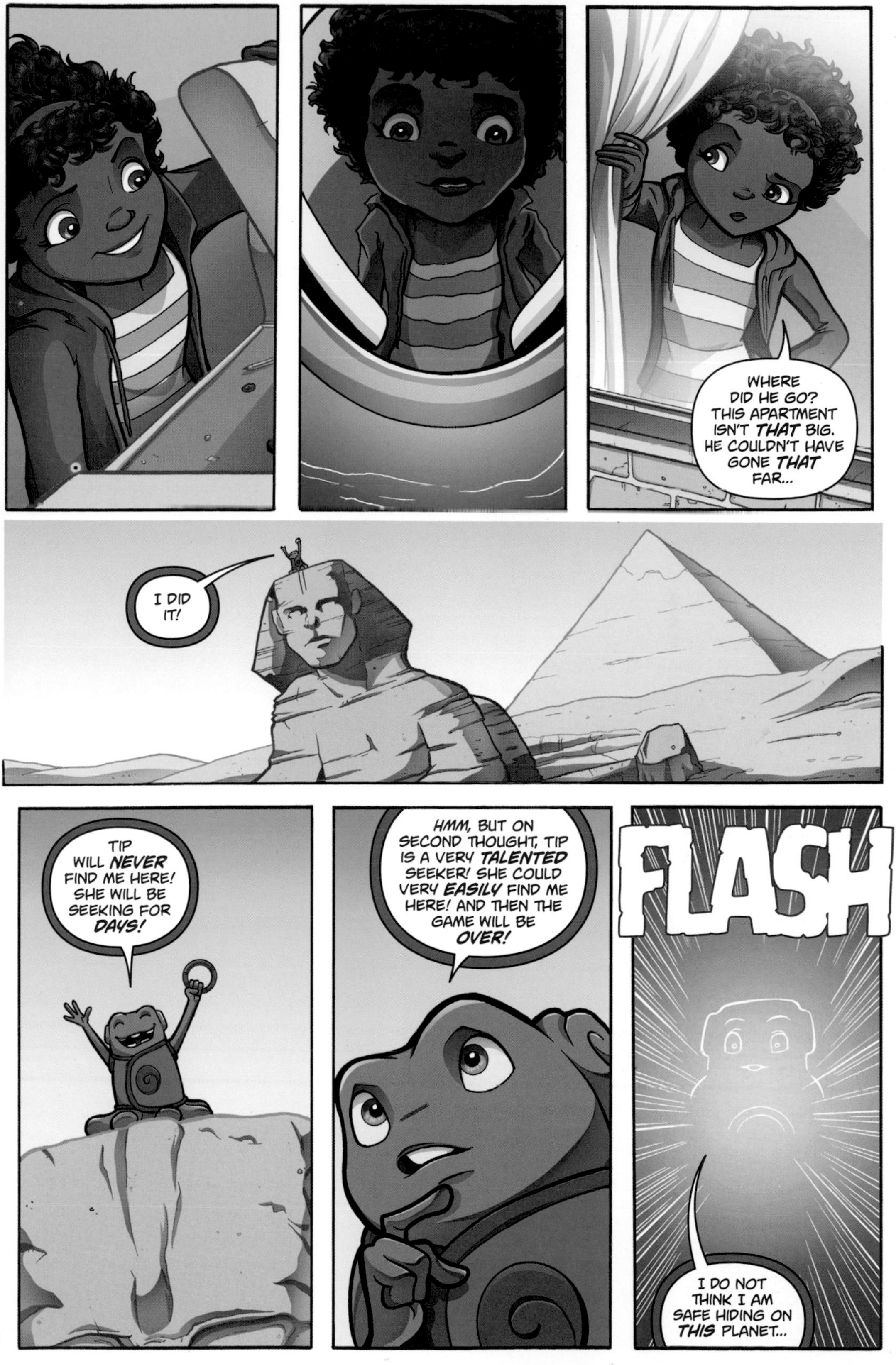

WHERE DID HE GO? THIS APARTMENT ISN'T THAT BIG. HE COULDN'T HAVE GONE THAT FAR...
I DID IT!
TIP WILL NEVER FIND ME HERE! SHE WILL BE SEEKING FOR DAYS!
HMM, BUT ON SECOND THOUGHT, TIP IS A VERY TALENTED SEEKER! SHE COULD VERY EASILY FIND ME HERE! AND THEN THE GAME WILL BE OVER!
FLASH
I DO NOT THINK I AM SAFE HIDING ON THIS PLANET...

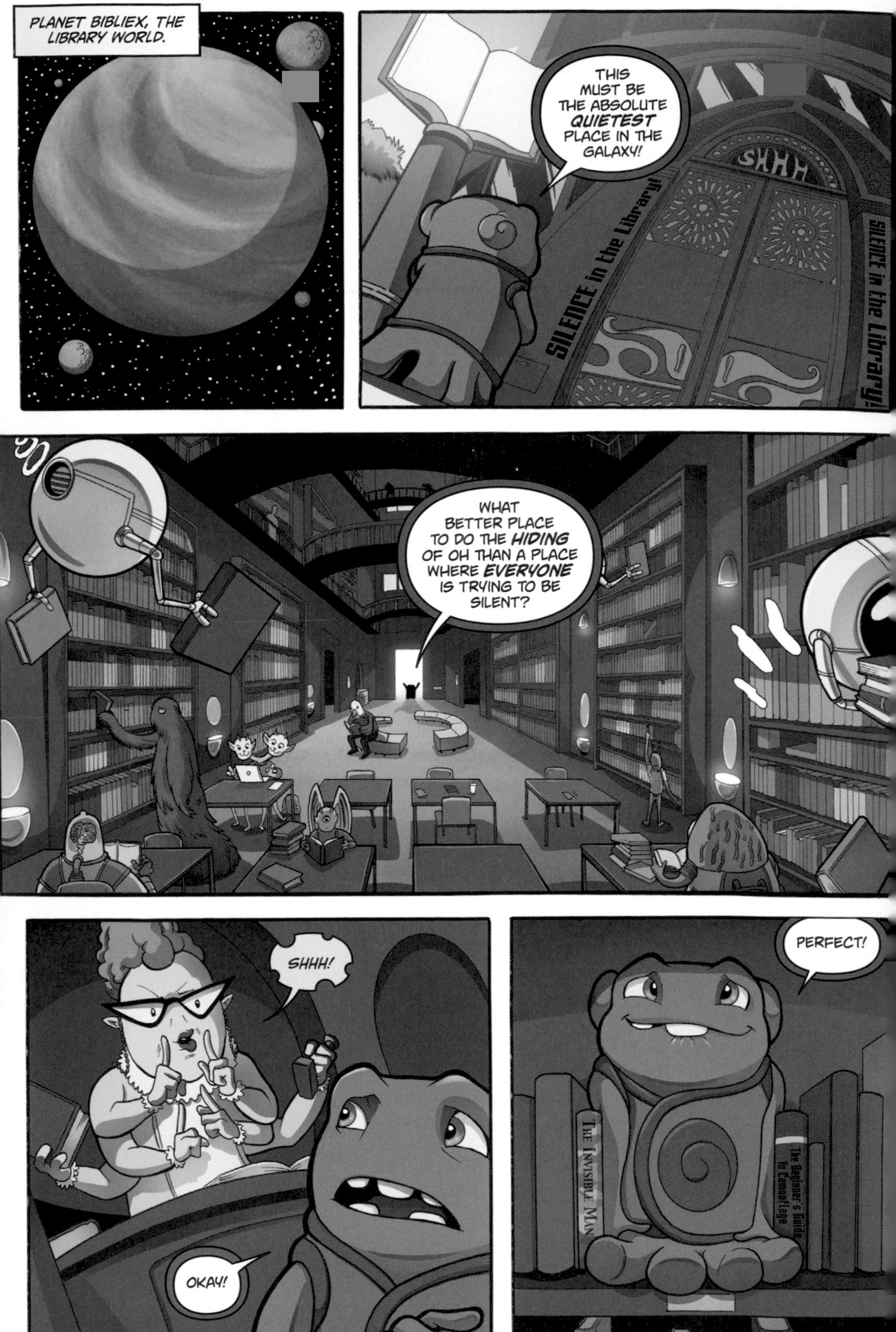
PLANET BIBLIEX, THE LIBRARY WORLD.
THIS MUST BE THE ABSOLUTE QUIETEST PLACE IN THE GALAXY!
SHHH
SILENCE in the Library!
SILENCE in the Library!
WHAT BETTER PLACE TO DO THE HIDING OF OH THAN A PLACE WHERE EVERYONE IS TRYING TO BE SILENT?
SHHH!
OKAY!
PERFECT!
THE INVISIBLE MAN
The Beginner's Guide To Camouflage

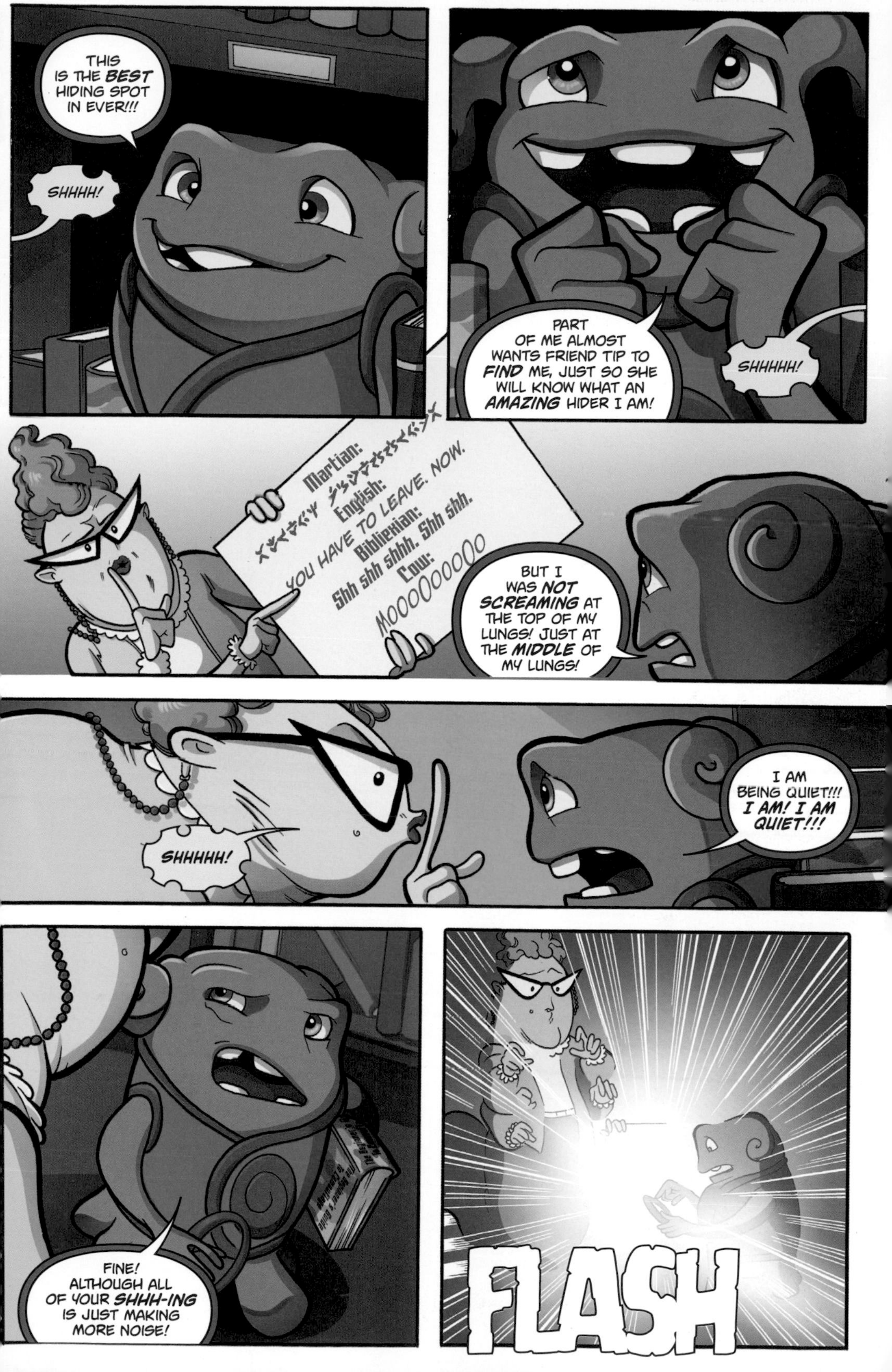
THIS IS THE BEST HIDING SPOT IN EVER!!!
SHHHH!
PART OF ME ALMOST WANTS FRIEND TIP TO FIND ME, JUST SO SHE WILL KNOW WHAT AN AMAZING HIDER I AM!
SHHHHH!
Martian:
English:
YOU HAVE TO LEAVE. NOW.
Bibliexian:
Shh shh shhh. Shh shh.
Cow:
MOOOOOOOOOO
BUT I WAS NOT SCREAMING AT THE TOP OF MY LUNGS! JUST AT THE MIDDLE OF MY LUNGS!
SHHHHH!
I AM BEING QUIET!!! I AM! I AM QUIET!!!
FINE! ALTHOUGH ALL OF YOUR SHHH-ING IS JUST MAKING MORE NOISE!
FLASH

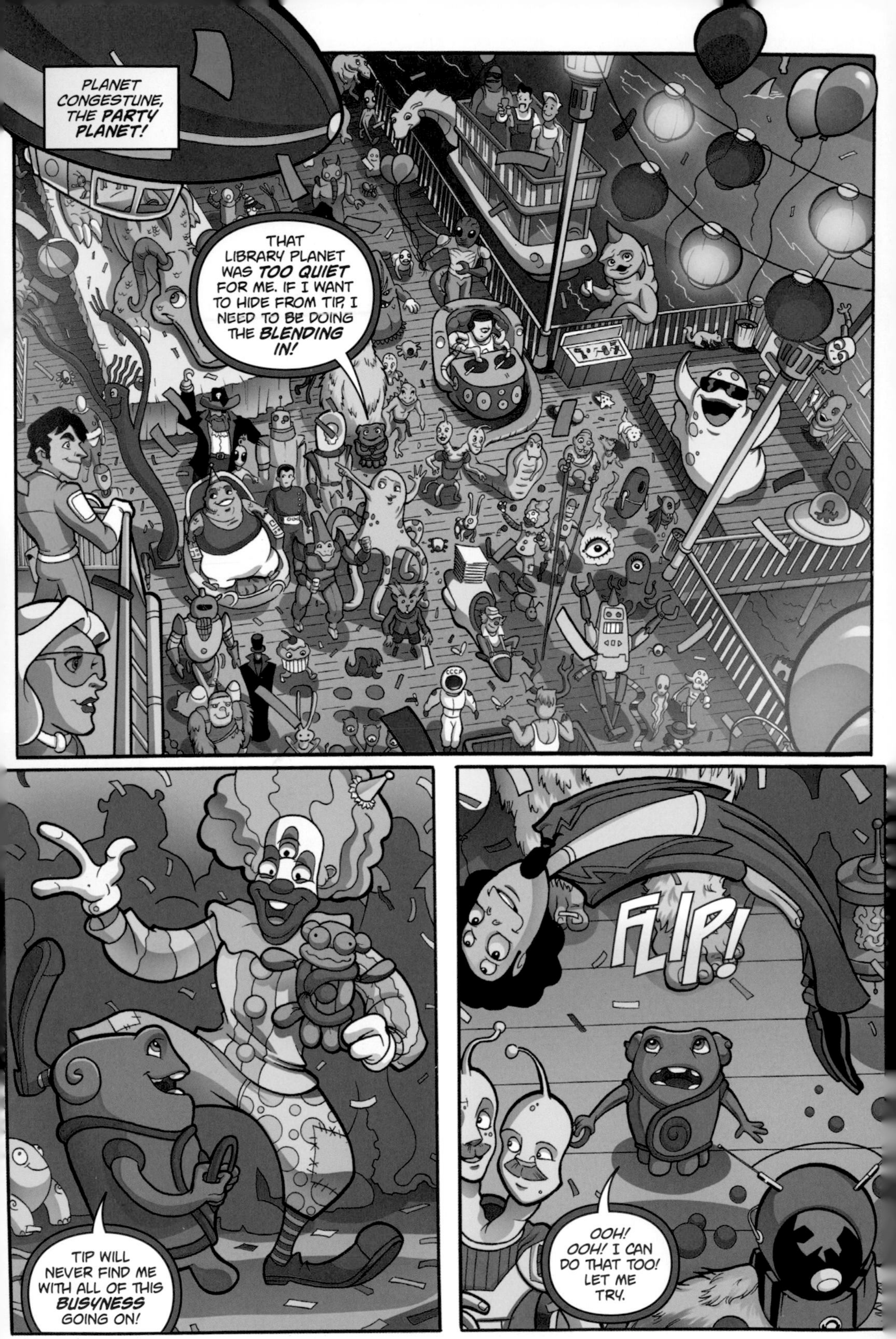
PLANET CONGESTUNE, THE PARTY PLANET!
THAT LIBRARY PLANET WAS TOO QUIET FOR ME. IF I WANT TO HIDE FROM TIP, I NEED TO BE DOING THE BLENDING IN!
CCCP
TIP WILL NEVER FIND ME WITH ALL OF THIS BUSYNESS GOING ON!
FLIP!
OOH! OOH! I CAN DO THAT TOO! LET ME TRY.

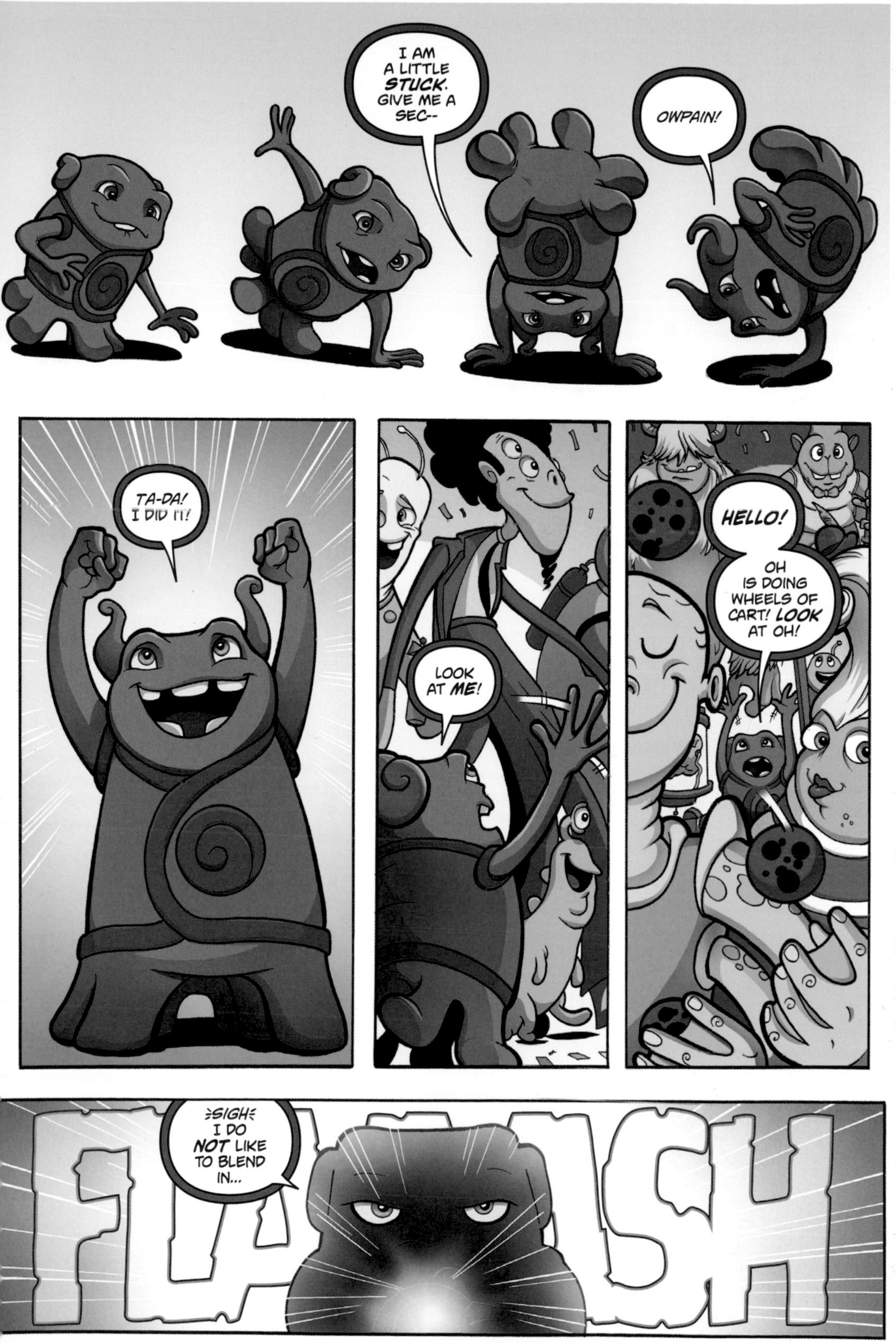
I AM A LITTLE STUCK. GIVE ME A SEC--
OWPAIN!
TA-DA! I DID IT!
LOOK AT ME!
HELLO!
OH IS DOING WHEELS OF CART! LOOK AT OH!
SIGH I DO NOT LIKE TO BLEND IN...

OKAY, OH. I GIVE UP. *YOU WIN!*

WE'VE LOOKED OVER THE ENTIRE APARTMENT. I'VE CHECKED ALL OF HIS FAVORITE HIDING PLACES: THE LAUNDRY SHOOT, THE RUBBISH BIN, ON TOP OF THE CUPBOARD.

WHERE COULD HE *BE*, PIG?

WAIT. WHAT'S *THIS?*

"USING A UNIQUE ENERGY TRAIL, THIS TELEPORTER CAN SEND YOU ACROSS A PLANET OR EVEN THE UNIVERSE. SERIOUSLY, THINK TWICE BEFORE USING THIS."

INFORMATION: USING A UNIQUE ENERGY TRAIL, THIS TELEPORTER CAN SEND YOU ACROSS A PLANET OR EVEN THE UNIVERSE. SERIOUSLY, THINK TWICE BEFORE USING THIS.

PIG, IF OH USED THIS *MACHINE...*

HE COULD BE *ANYWHERE!*

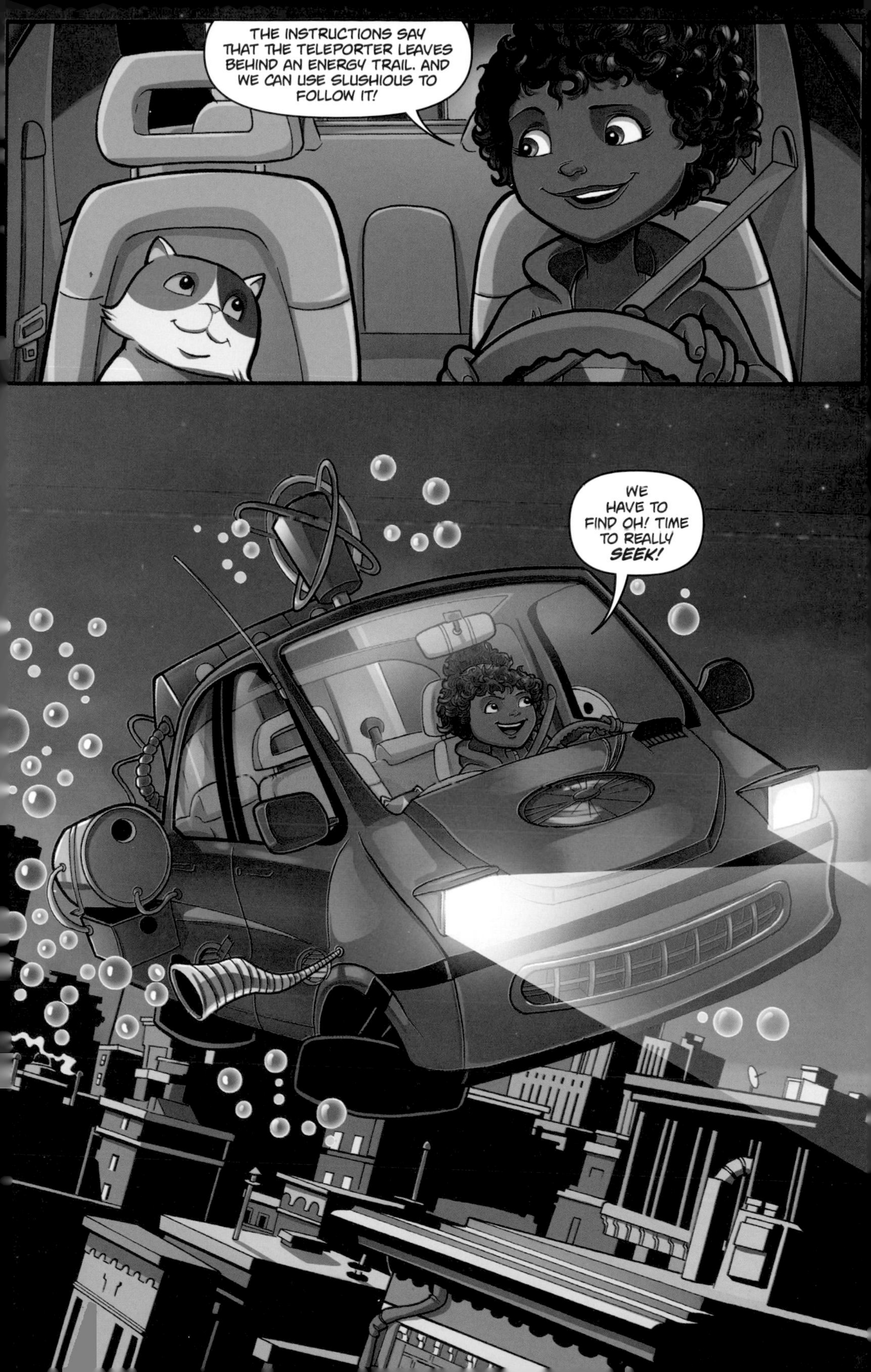
THE INSTRUCTIONS SAY THAT THE TELEPORTER LEAVES BEHIND AN ENERGY TRAIL. AND WE CAN USE SLUSHIOUS TO FOLLOW IT!
WE HAVE TO FIND OH! TIME TO REALLY SEEK!

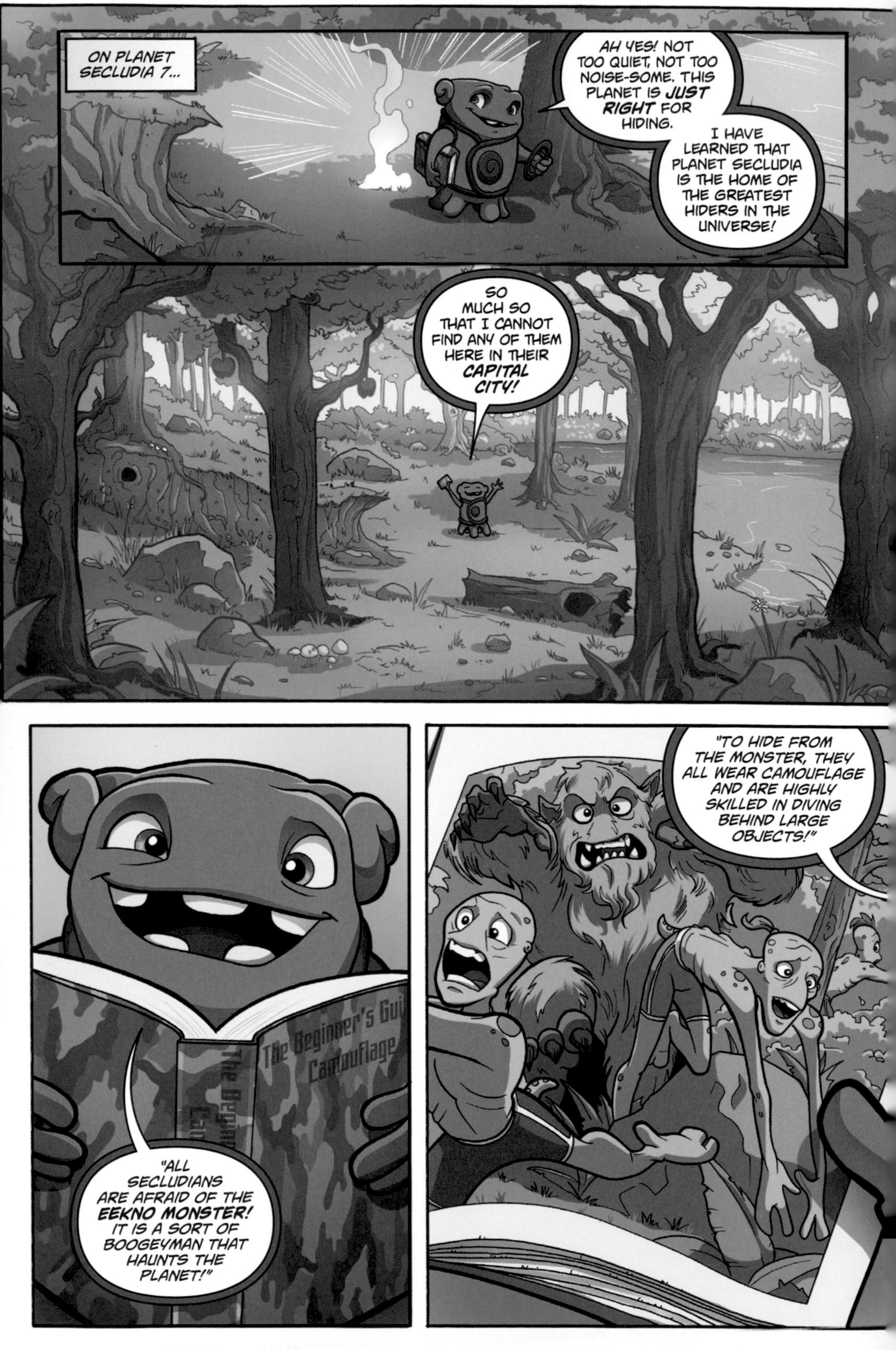
ON PLANET SECLUDIA 7...
AH YES! NOT TOO QUIET, NOT TOO NOISE-SOME. THIS PLANET IS **JUST RIGHT** FOR HIDING.
I HAVE LEARNED THAT PLANET SECLUDIA IS THE HOME OF THE GREATEST HIDERS IN THE UNIVERSE!
SO MUCH SO THAT I CANNOT FIND ANY OF THEM HERE IN THEIR **CAPITAL CITY!**
The Beginner's Gui Camouflage
"ALL SECLUDIANS ARE AFRAID OF THE **EEKNO MONSTER!** IT IS A SORT OF BOOGEYMAN THAT HAUNTS THE PLANET!"
"TO HIDE FROM THE MONSTER, THEY ALL WEAR CAMOUFLAGE AND ARE HIGHLY SKILLED IN DIVING BEHIND LARGE OBJECTS!"

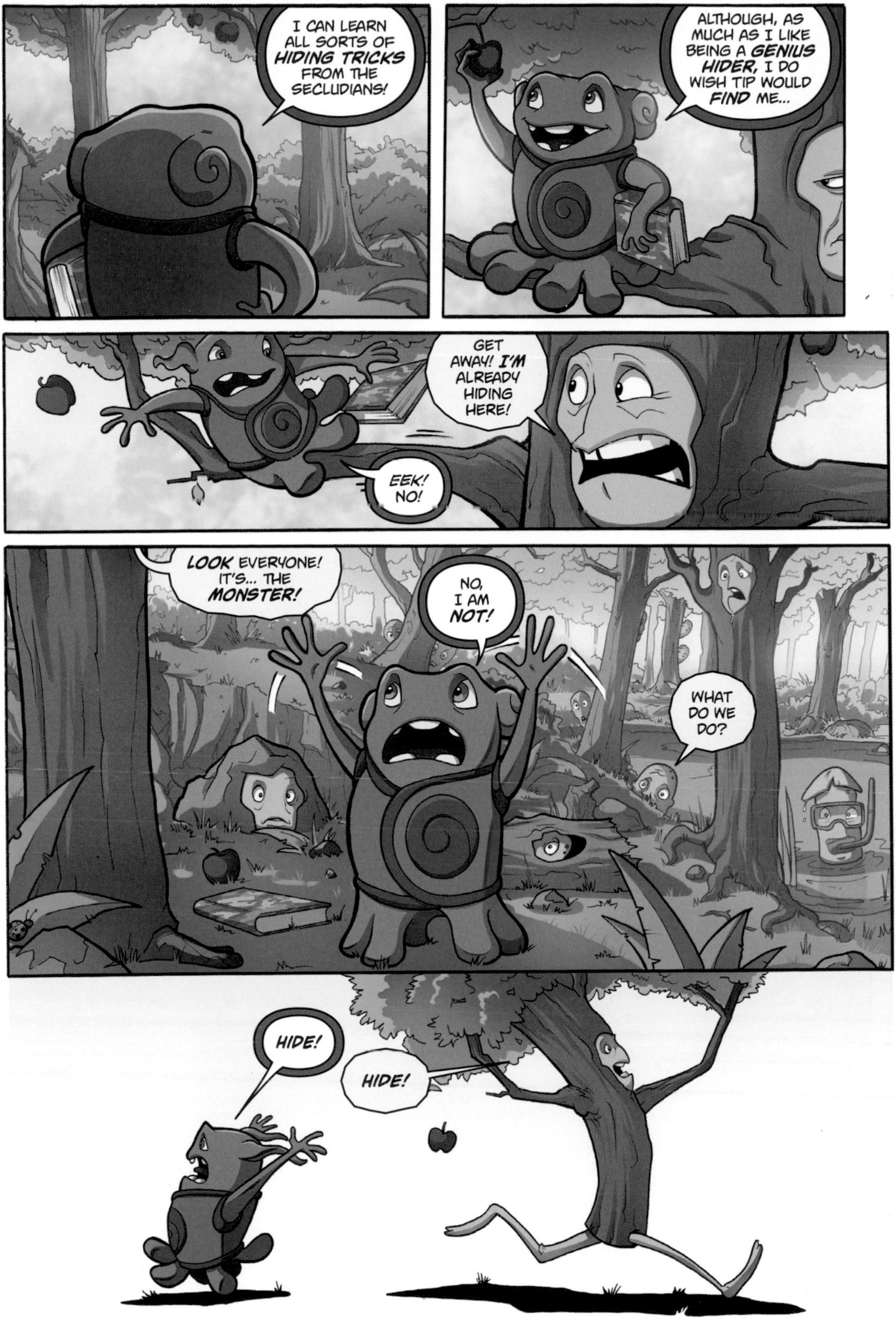
I CAN LEARN ALL SORTS OF HIDING TRICKS FROM THE SECLUDIANS!
ALTHOUGH, AS MUCH AS I LIKE BEING A GENIUS HIDER, I DO WISH TIP WOULD FIND ME...
GET AWAY! I'M ALREADY HIDING HERE!
EEK! NO!
LOOK EVERYONE! IT'S... THE MONSTER!
NO, I AM NOT!
WHAT DO WE DO?
HIDE!
HIDE!

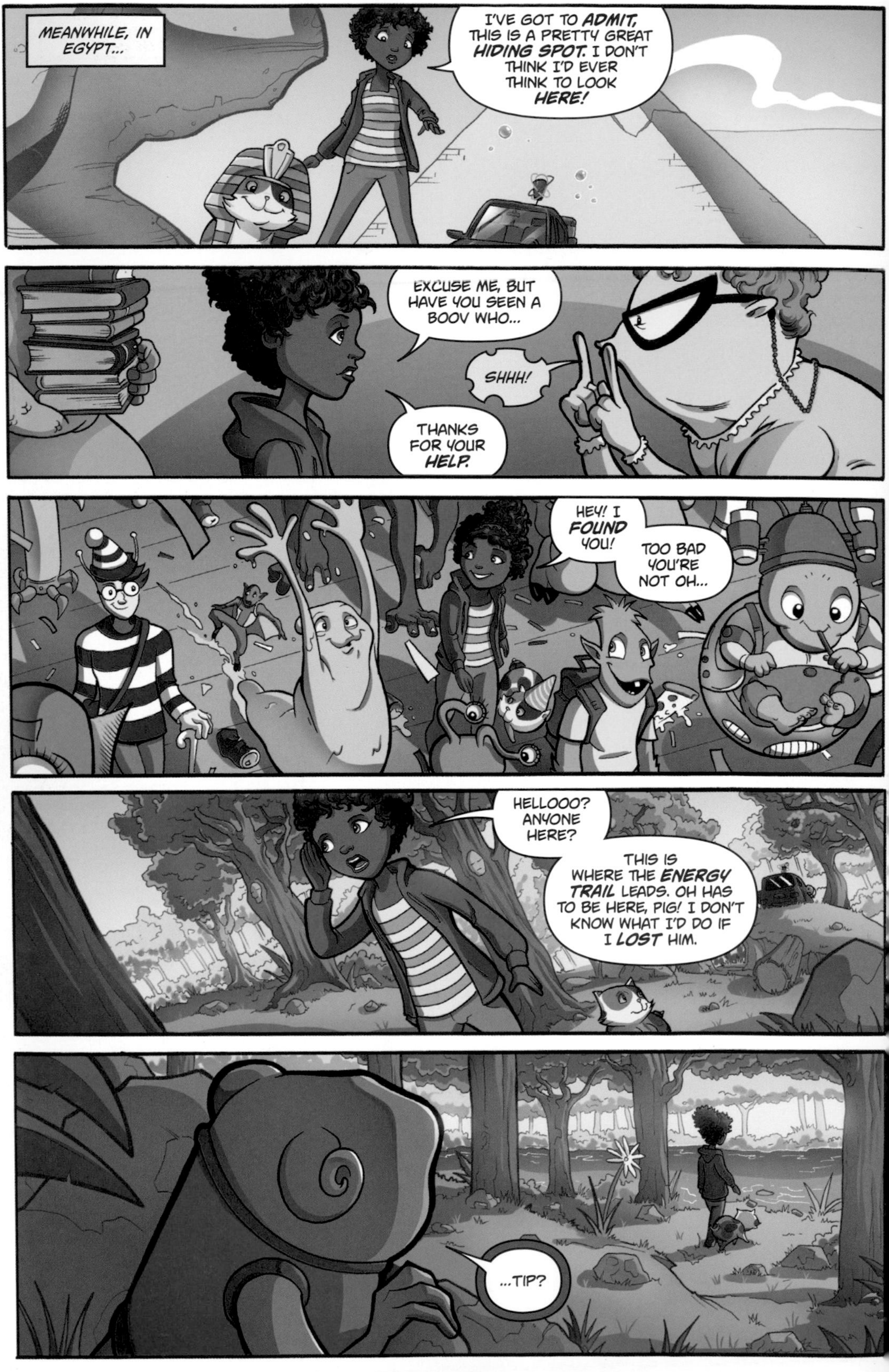
MEANWHILE, IN EGYPT...
I'VE GOT TO ADMIT, THIS IS A PRETTY GREAT HIDING SPOT. I DON'T THINK I'D EVER THINK TO LOOK HERE!
EXCUSE ME, BUT HAVE YOU SEEN A BOOV WHO...
SHHH!
THANKS FOR YOUR HELP.
HEY! I FOUND YOU!
TOO BAD YOU'RE NOT OH...
HELLOOO? ANYONE HERE?
THIS IS WHERE THE ENERGY TRAIL LEADS. OH HAS TO BE HERE, PIG! I DON'T KNOW WHAT I'D DO IF I LOST HIM.
...TIP?

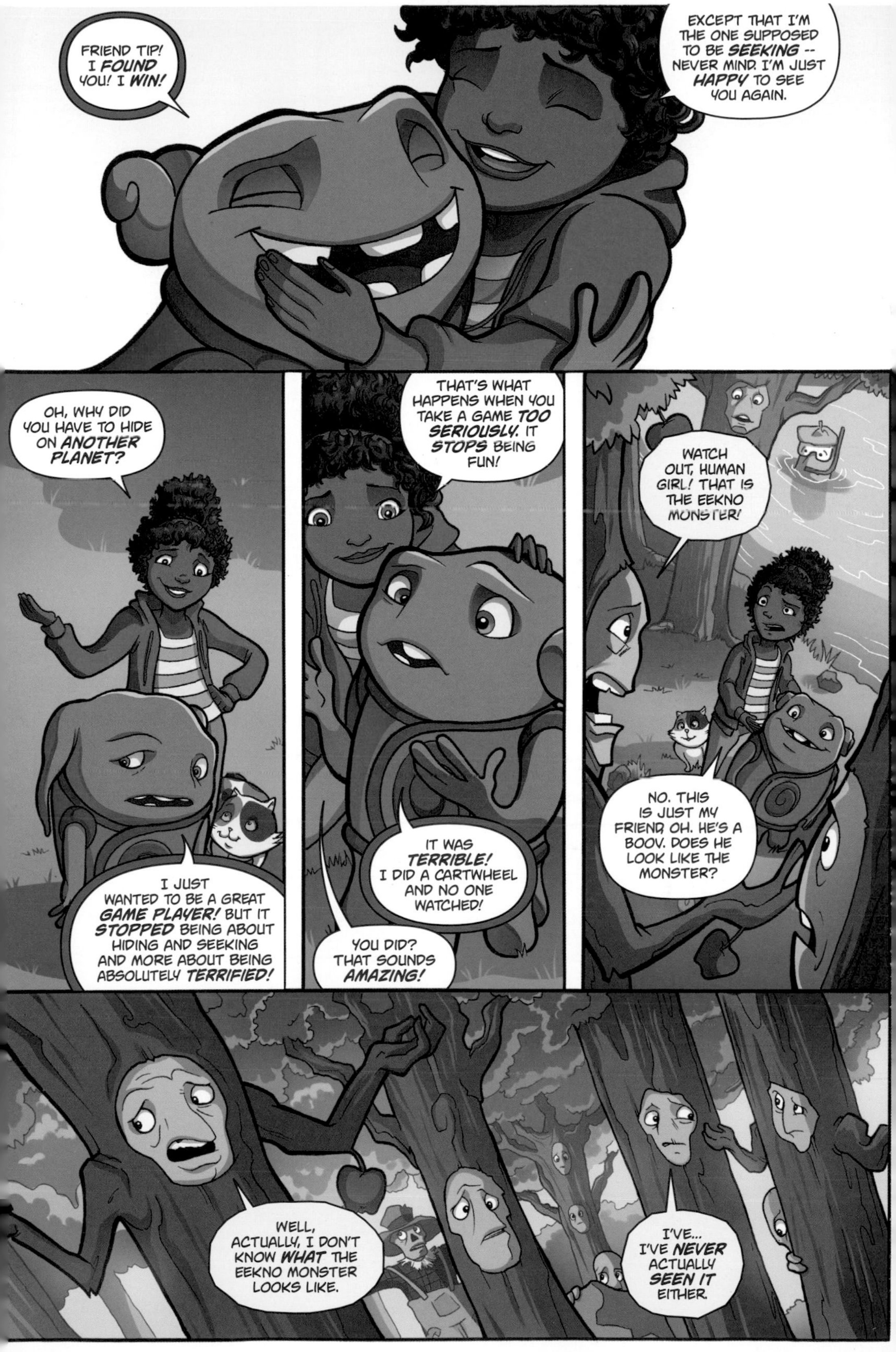

FRIEND TIP! I FOUND YOU! I WIN!
EXCEPT THAT I'M THE ONE SUPPOSED TO BE SEEKING -- NEVER MIND. I'M JUST HAPPY TO SEE YOU AGAIN.
OH, WHY DID YOU HAVE TO HIDE ON ANOTHER PLANET?
I JUST WANTED TO BE A GREAT GAME PLAYER! BUT IT STOPPED BEING ABOUT HIDING AND SEEKING AND MORE ABOUT BEING ABSOLUTELY TERRIFIED!
THAT'S WHAT HAPPENS WHEN YOU TAKE A GAME TOO SERIOUSLY. IT STOPS BEING FUN!
IT WAS TERRIBLE! I DID A CARTWHEEL AND NO ONE WATCHED!
YOU DID? THAT SOUNDS AMAZING!
WATCH OUT, HUMAN GIRL! THAT IS THE EEKNO MONSTER!
NO. THIS IS JUST MY FRIEND, OH. HE'S A BOOV. DOES HE LOOK LIKE THE MONSTER?
WELL, ACTUALLY, I DON'T KNOW WHAT THE EEKNO MONSTER LOOKS LIKE.
I'VE... I'VE NEVER ACTUALLY SEEN IT EITHER.

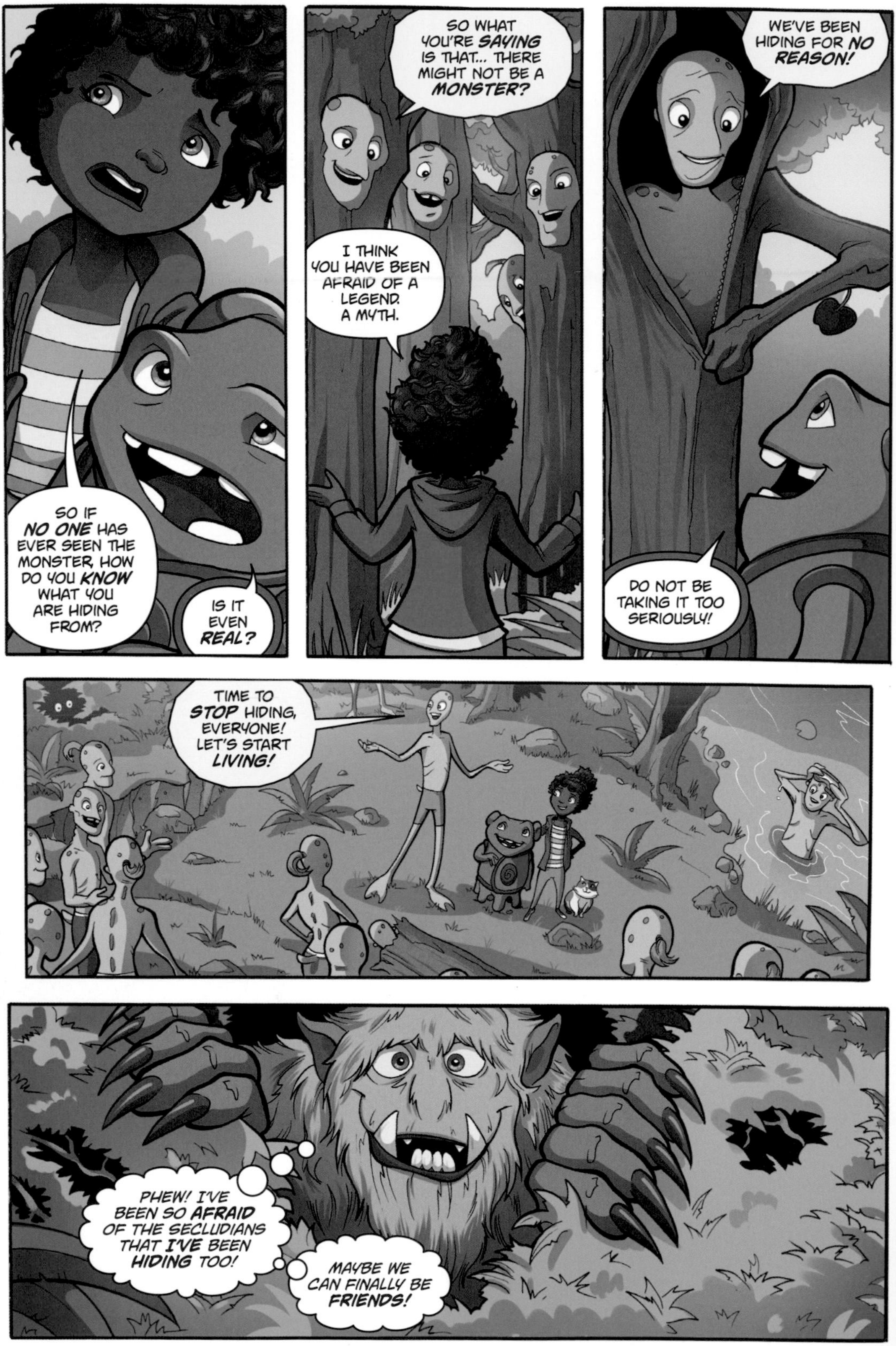

SO IF NO ONE HAS EVER SEEN THE MONSTER, HOW DO YOU KNOW WHAT YOU ARE HIDING FROM?
IS IT EVEN REAL?
SO WHAT YOU'RE SAYING IS THAT... THERE MIGHT NOT BE A MONSTER?
I THINK YOU HAVE BEEN AFRAID OF A LEGEND. A MYTH.
WE'VE BEEN HIDING FOR NO REASON!
DO NOT BE TAKING IT TOO SERIOUSLY!
TIME TO STOP HIDING, EVERYONE! LET'S START LIVING!
PHEW! I'VE BEEN SO AFRAID OF THE SECLUDIANS THAT I'VE BEEN HIDING TOO!
MAYBE WE CAN FINALLY BE FRIENDS!

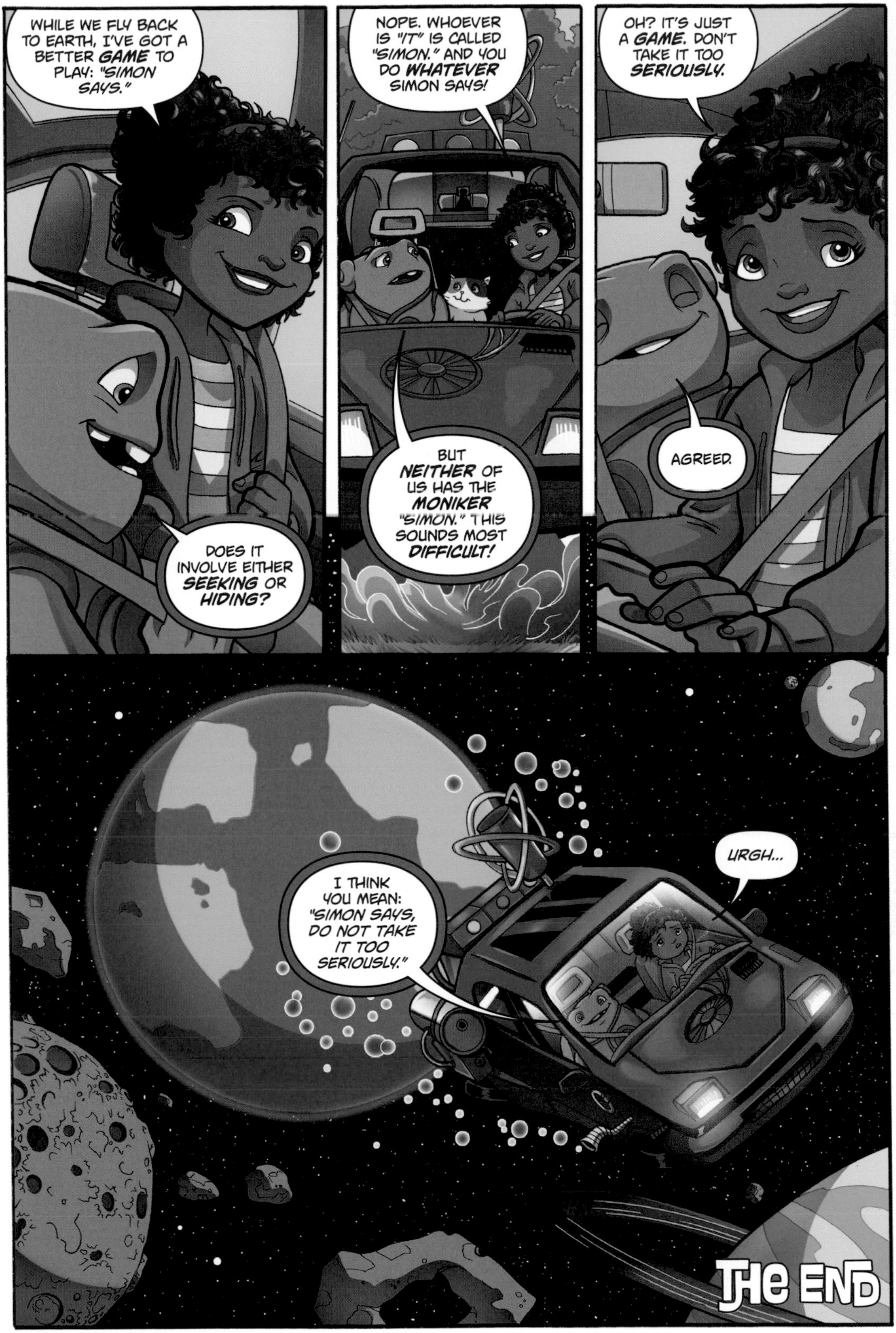
WHILE WE FLY BACK TO EARTH, I'VE GOT A BETTER GAME TO PLAY: "SIMON SAYS."
DOES IT INVOLVE EITHER SEEKING OR HIDING?
NOPE. WHOEVER IS "IT" IS CALLED "SIMON." AND YOU DO WHATEVER SIMON SAYS!
BUT NEITHER OF US HAS THE MONIKER "SIMON." THIS SOUNDS MOST DIFFICULT!
OH? IT'S JUST A GAME. DON'T TAKE IT TOO SERIOUSLY.
AGREED.
I THINK YOU MEAN: "SIMON SAYS, DO NOT TAKE IT TOO SERIOUSLY."
URGH...
THE END

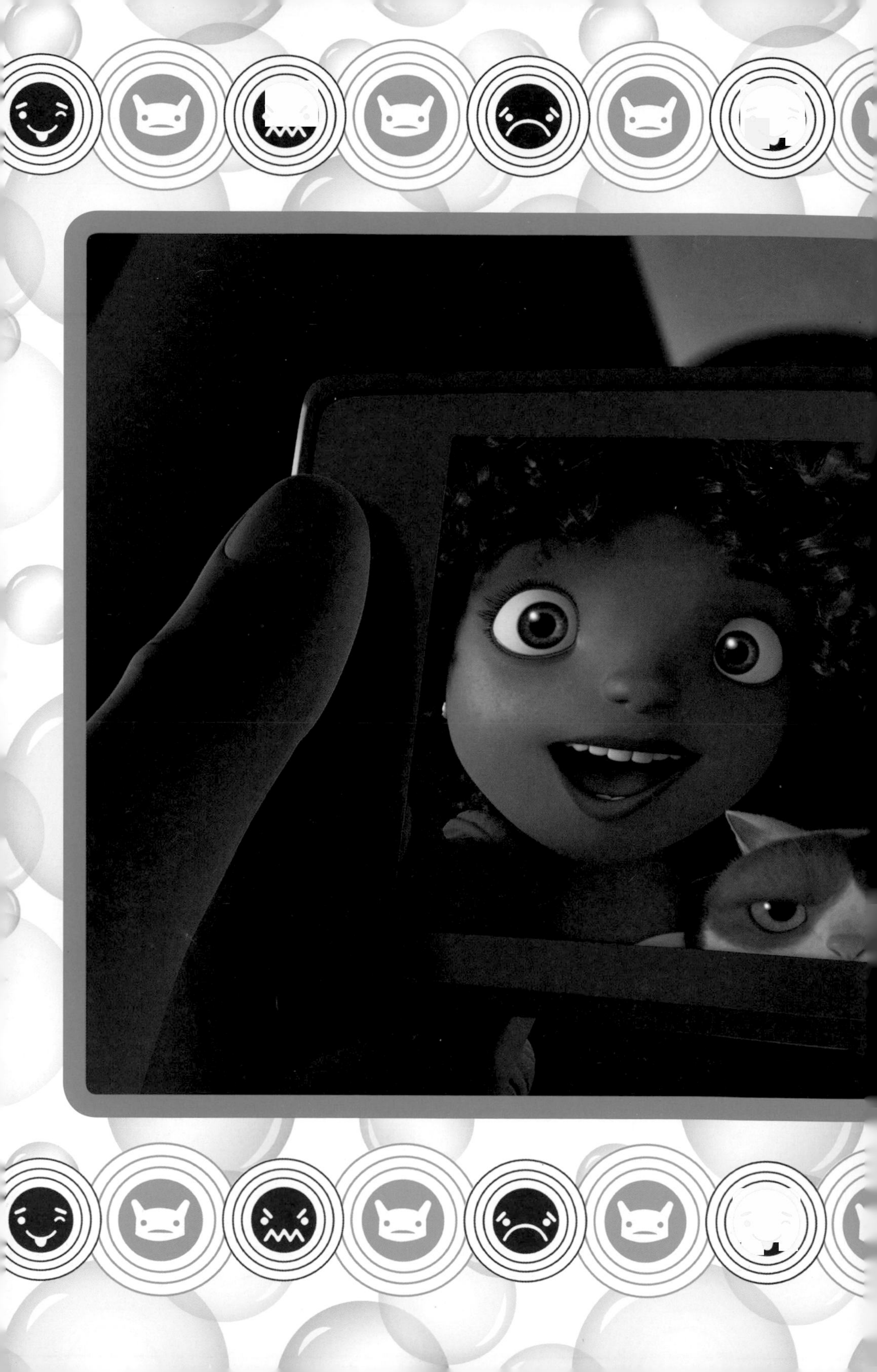

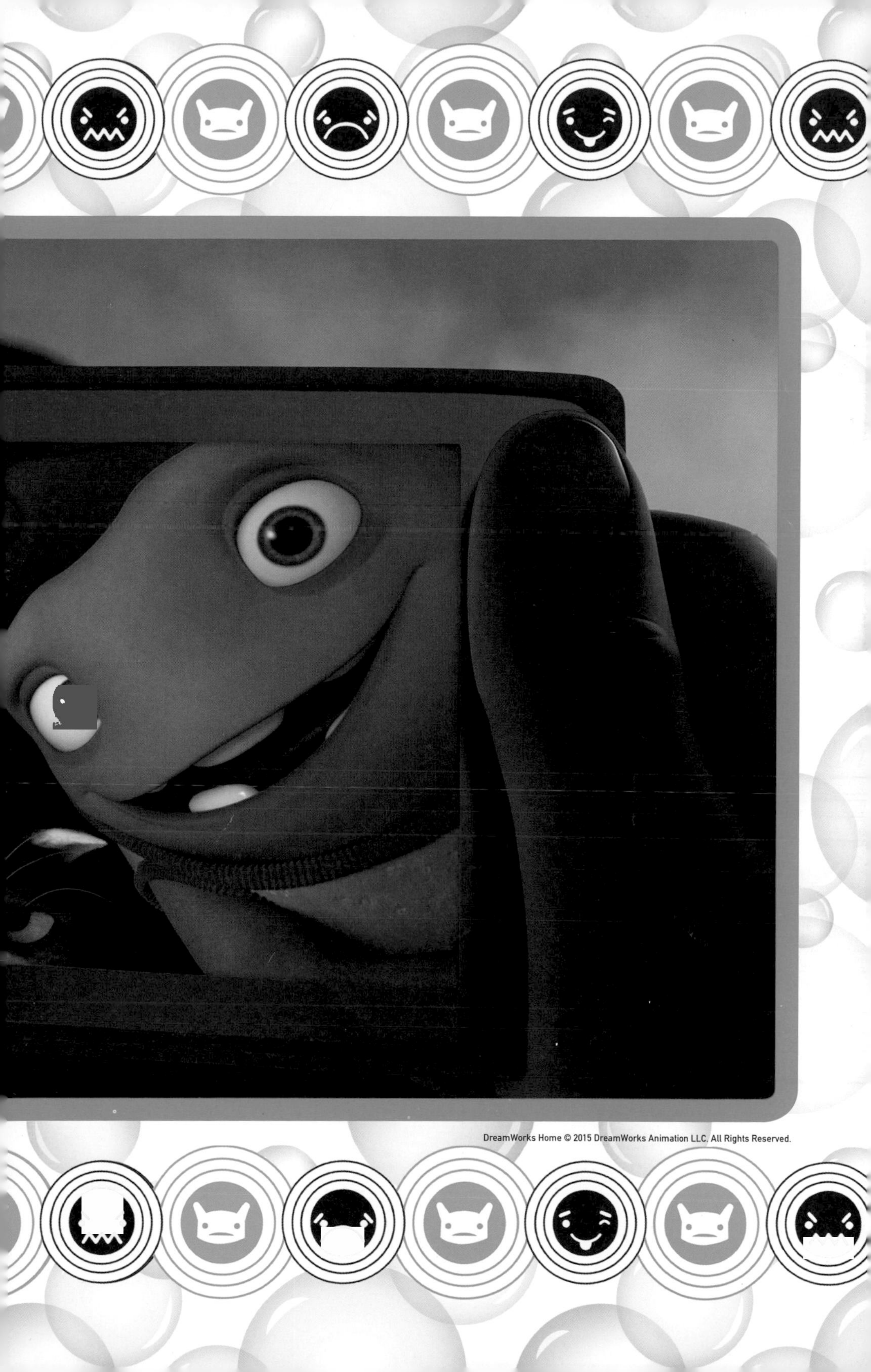

THE FUNNY PAGES

WRITER Martin Eden
ART Alex Dalton
COLORS Phil Elliott
LETTERS Jim Campbell

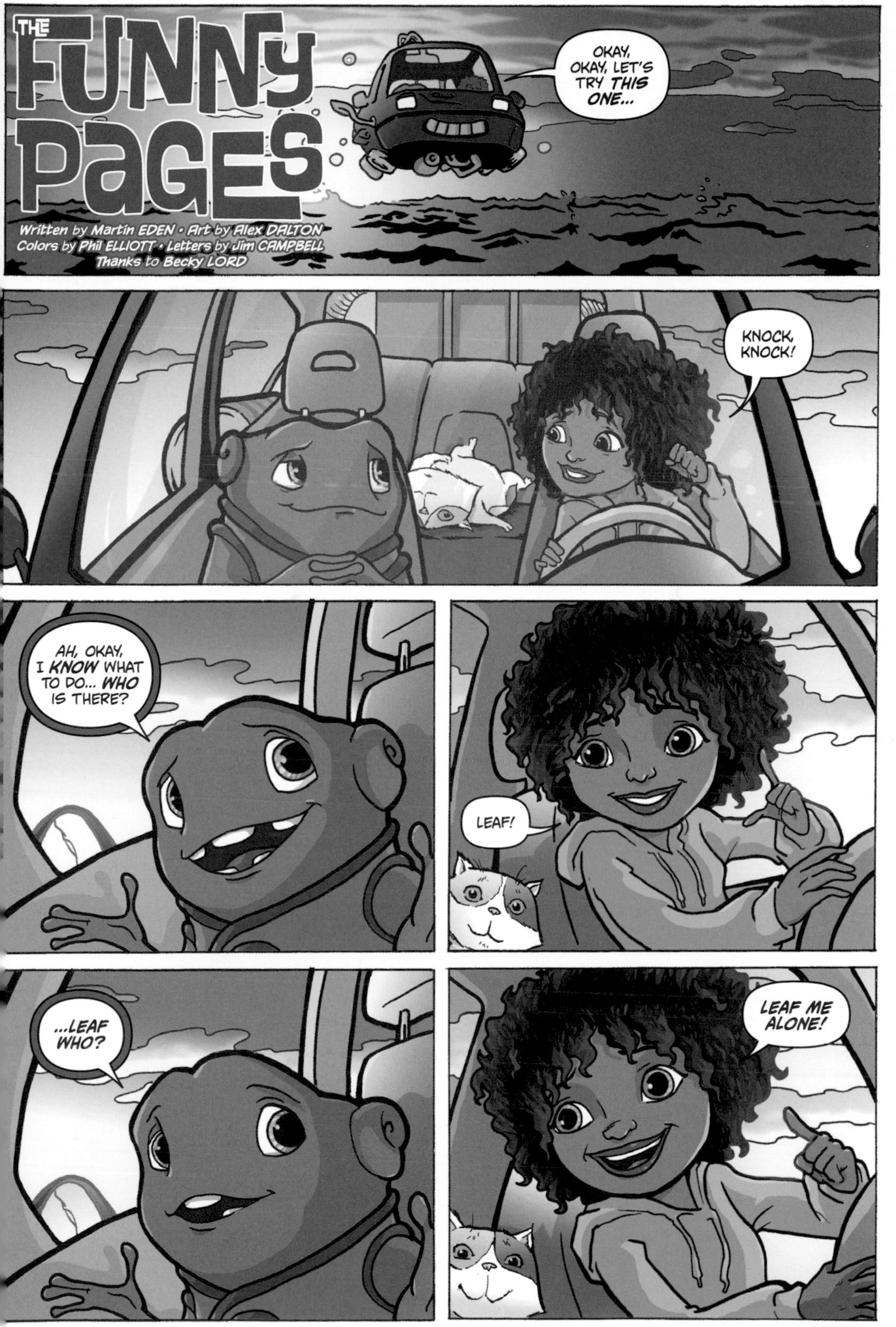
THE FUNNY PAGES
OKAY, OKAY, LET'S TRY THIS ONE...
Written by Martin EDEN • Art by Alex DALTON
Colors by Phil ELLIOTT • Letters by Jim CAMPBELL
Thanks to Becky LORD
KNOCK, KNOCK!
AH, OKAY, I KNOW WHAT TO DO... WHO IS THERE?
LEAF!
...LEAF WHO?
LEAF ME ALONE!

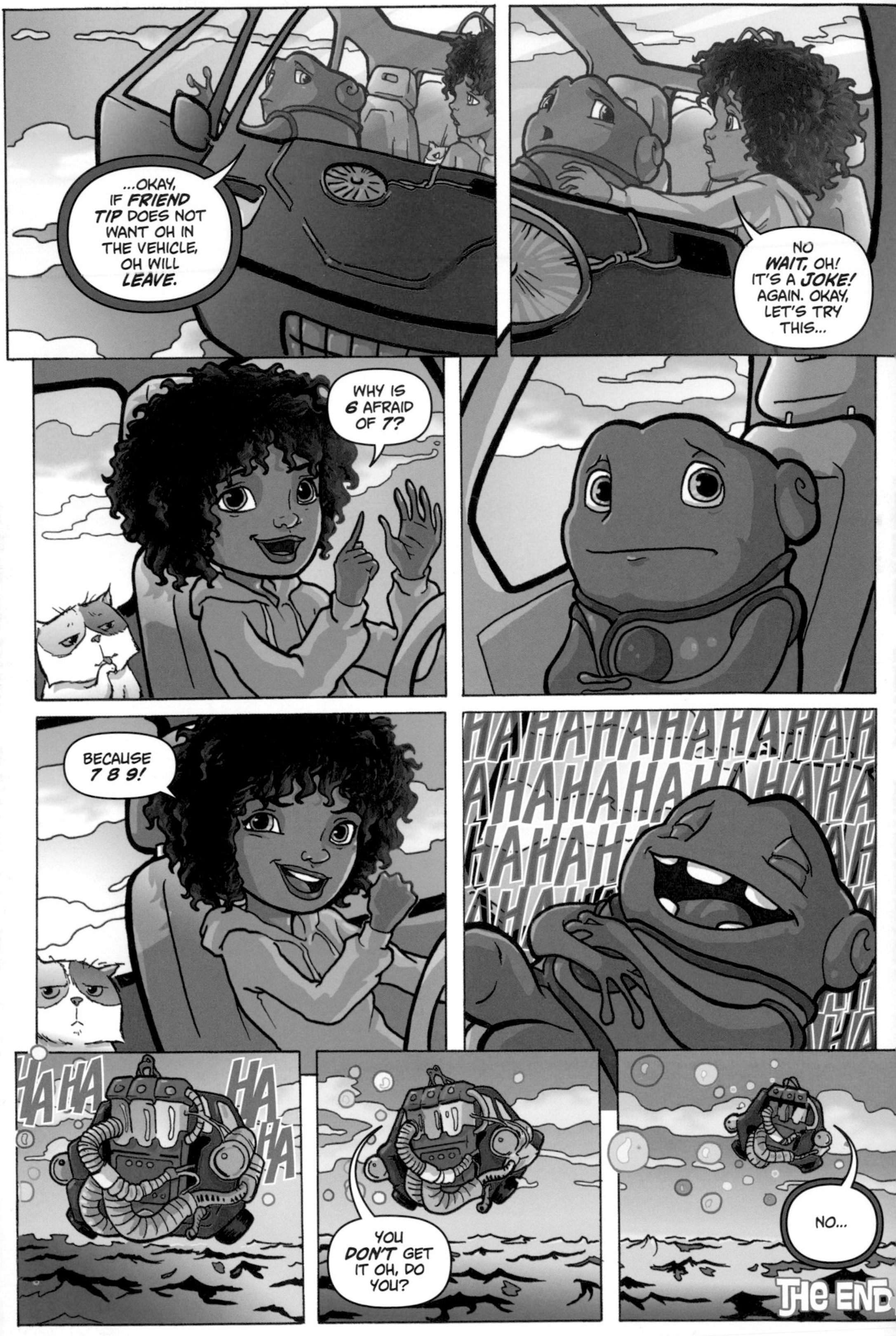
...OKAY, IF FRIEND TIP DOES NOT WANT OH IN THE VEHICLE, OH WILL LEAVE.
NO WAIT, OH! IT'S A JOKE! AGAIN. OKAY, LET'S TRY THIS...
WHY IS 6 AFRAID OF 7?
BECAUSE 7 8 9!
HAHAHAHAHAHAHAHAHAH
HA HA
HA HA
YOU DON'T GET IT OH, DO YOU?
NO...
THE END

EXTRACT FROM THE BOOV COMPREHENSIVE INFORMATION GUIDE TO HUMANS

(Or 'How to Deal with a Simple and Backwards Race')

PAGE 356

PARENTS

Whereas young Boov are kept in a warming oven, many humanschildren have a 'mother' and 'father.' These seem to be very important humanspersons and, if separated, humanschildren often travel varying distances to visit them.

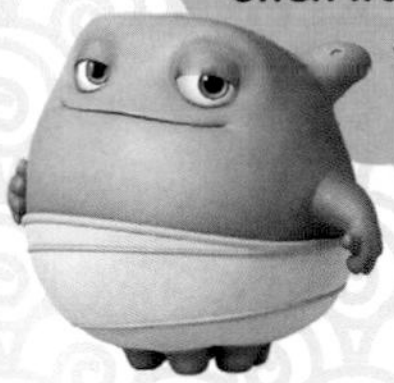

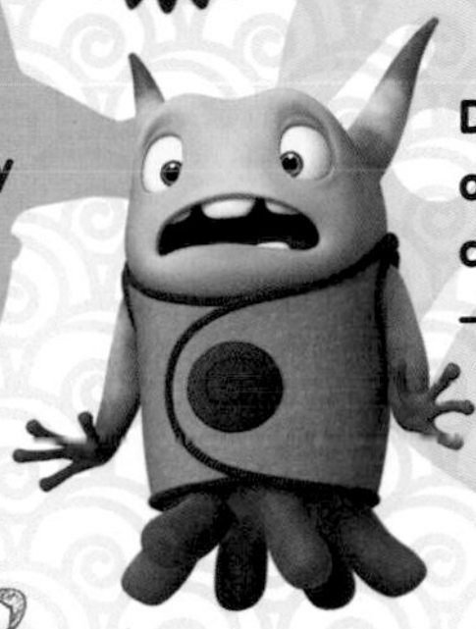

PUBLIC TOILETS

Do not eat the blue mints or drink the lemonade. Be careful of the gust machine – it can blow a small Boov over.

FACT #2317:

Humanspersons care about other humanspersons! Boov do not care about each other in any way.

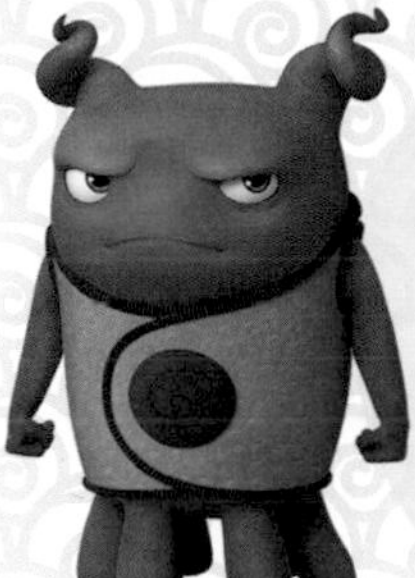

MUSIC

Whenever music is played, humans immediately stop what they are doing and dance around. Warning: Dancing may cause a Boov to overheat his or her core.

PETS

Humans house small animals for company. These animals include cats, dogs, snakes, gerbils, spiders and babies. The animals are not kept for milk like we thought at first.

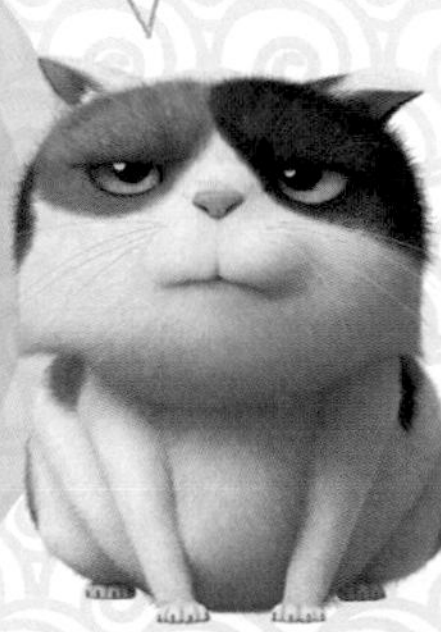

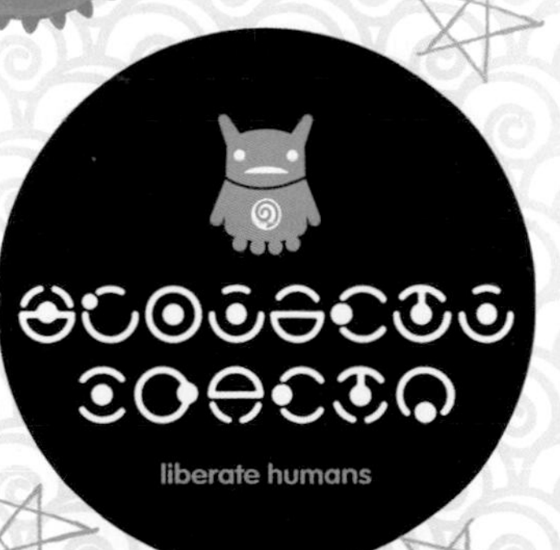
liberate humans

By Becky Lord

OH EMPLOYMENT

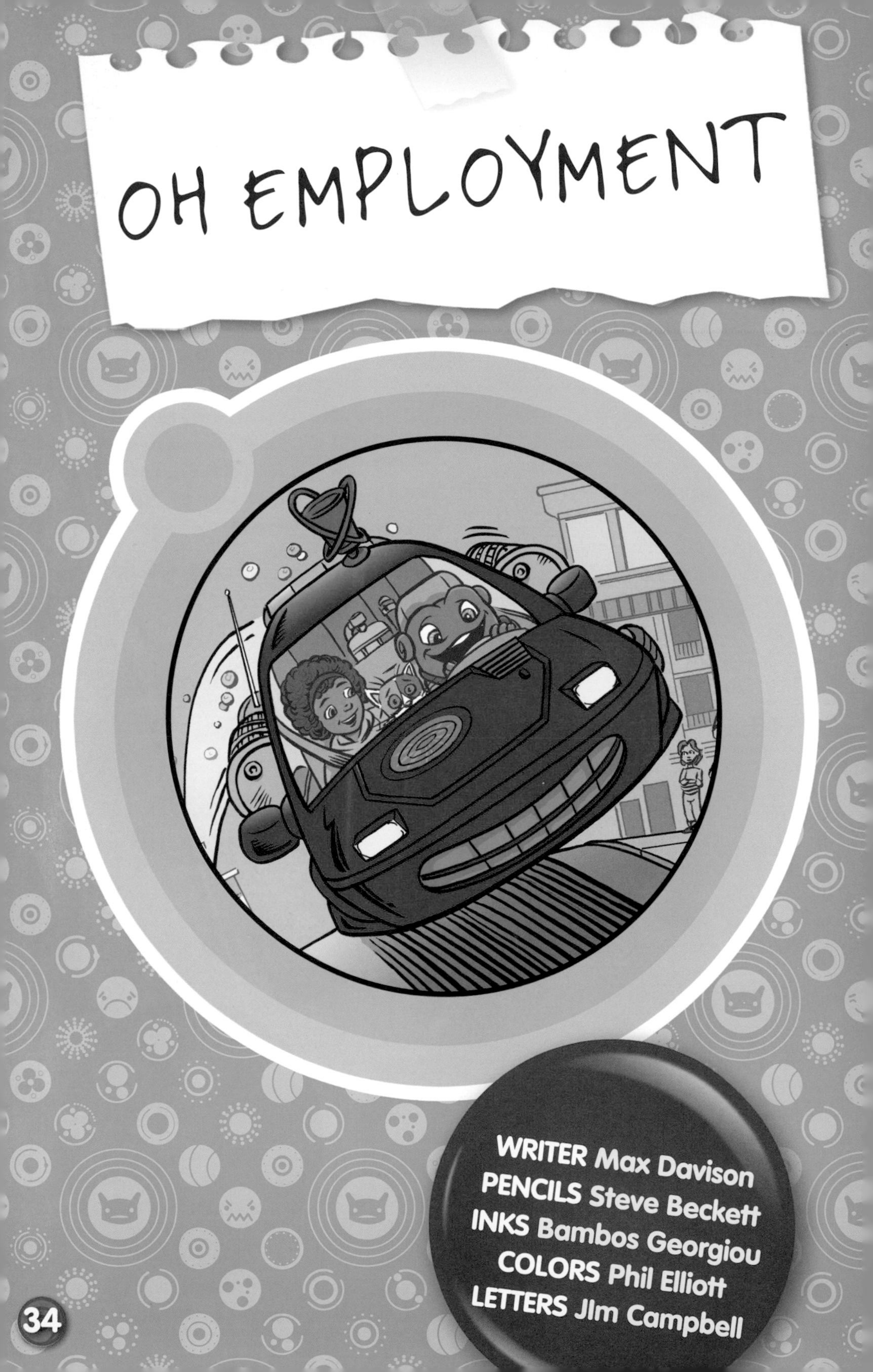

WRITER Max Davison
PENCILS Steve Beckett
INKS Bambos Georgiou
COLORS Phil Elliott
LETTERS Jim Campbell

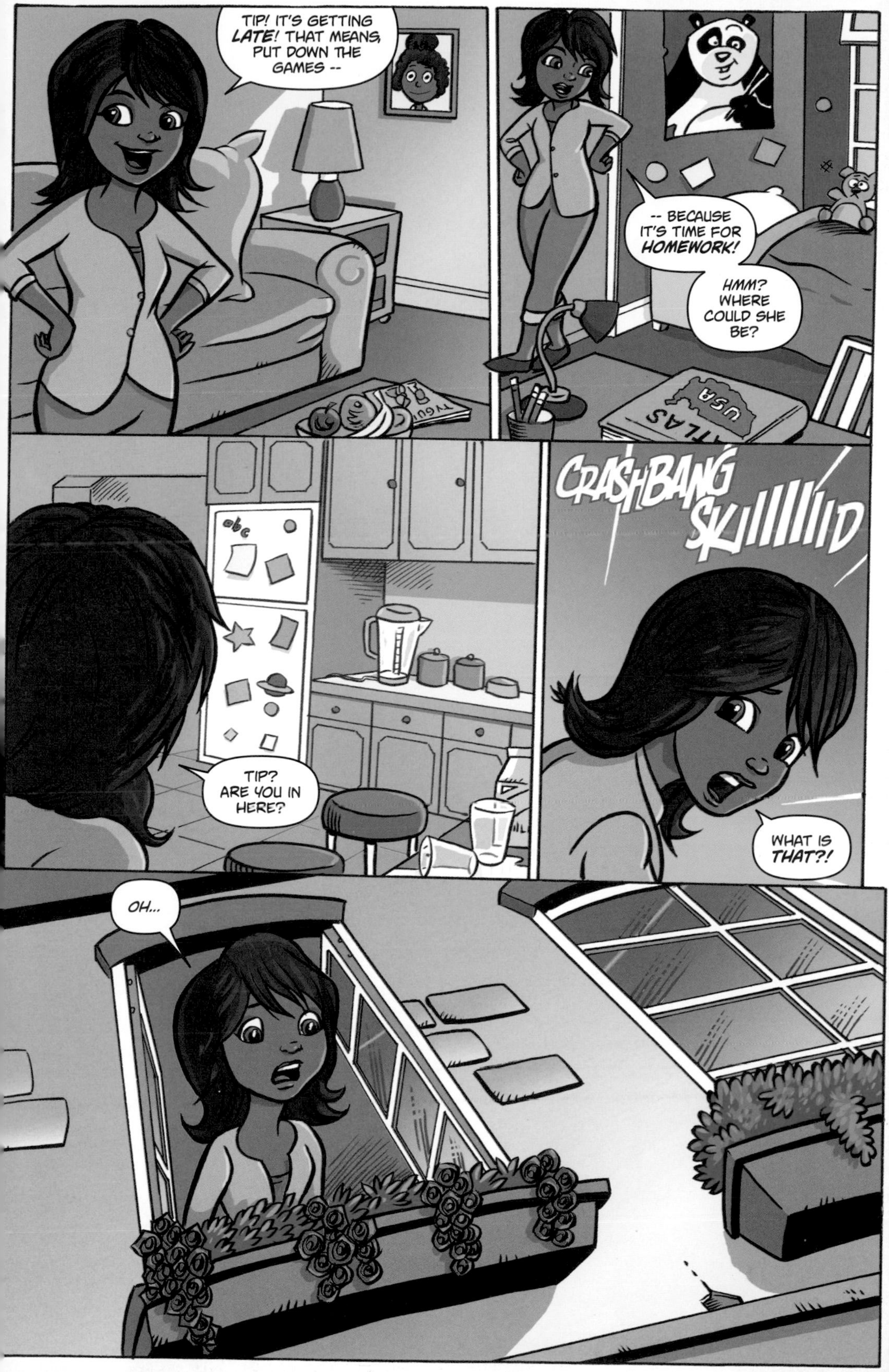
TIP! IT'S GETTING LATE! THAT MEANS, PUT DOWN THE GAMES --
-- BECAUSE IT'S TIME FOR HOMEWORK!
HMM? WHERE COULD SHE BE?
USA
TIP? ARE YOU IN HERE?
CRASHBANG
SKIIIIIIID
WHAT IS THAT?!
OH...

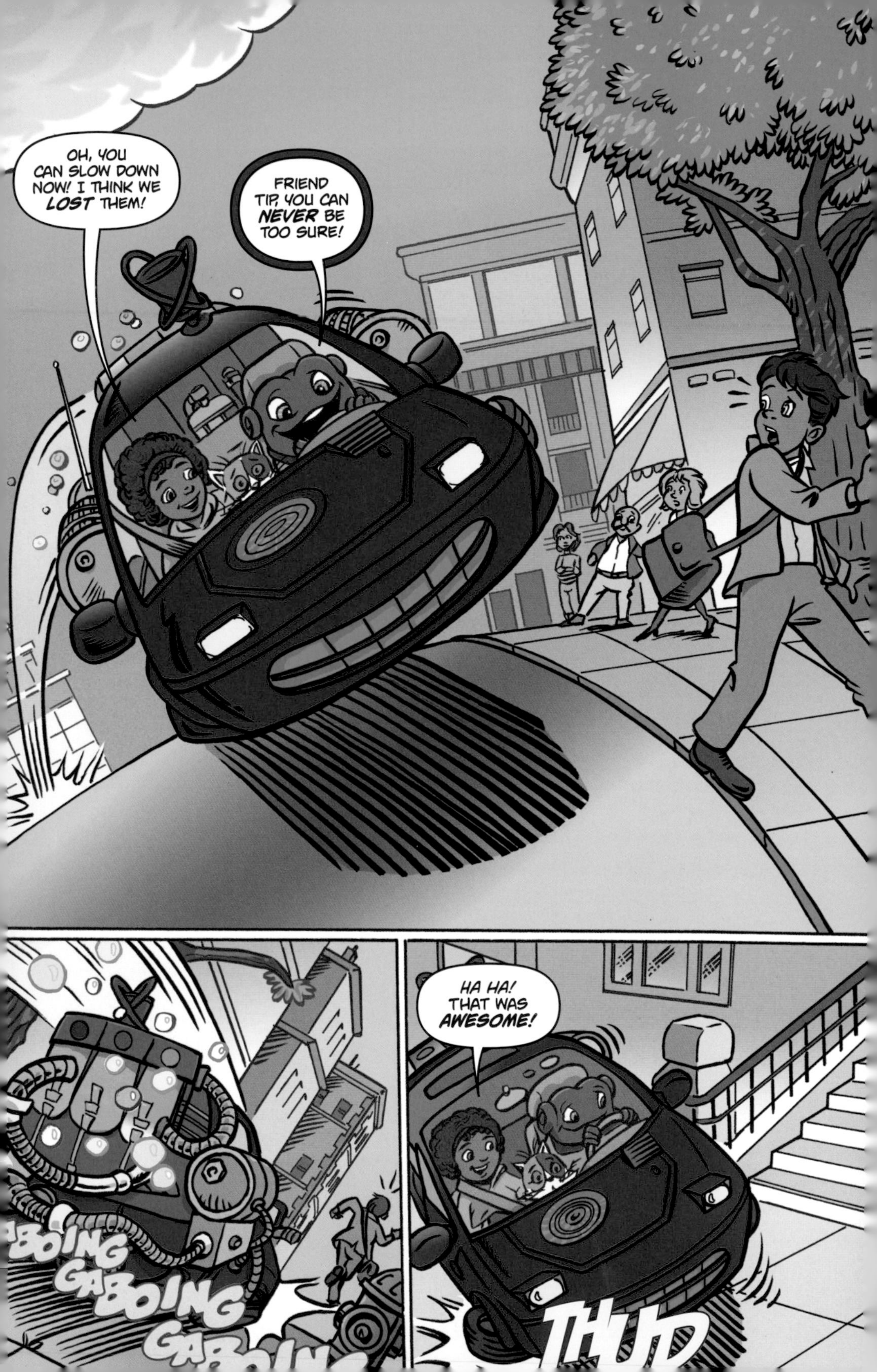
OH, YOU CAN SLOW DOWN NOW! I THINK WE **LOST** THEM!
FRIEND TIP, YOU CAN **NEVER** BE TOO SURE!
BOING GABOING GABOING
HA HA! THAT WAS **AWESOME!**
THUD

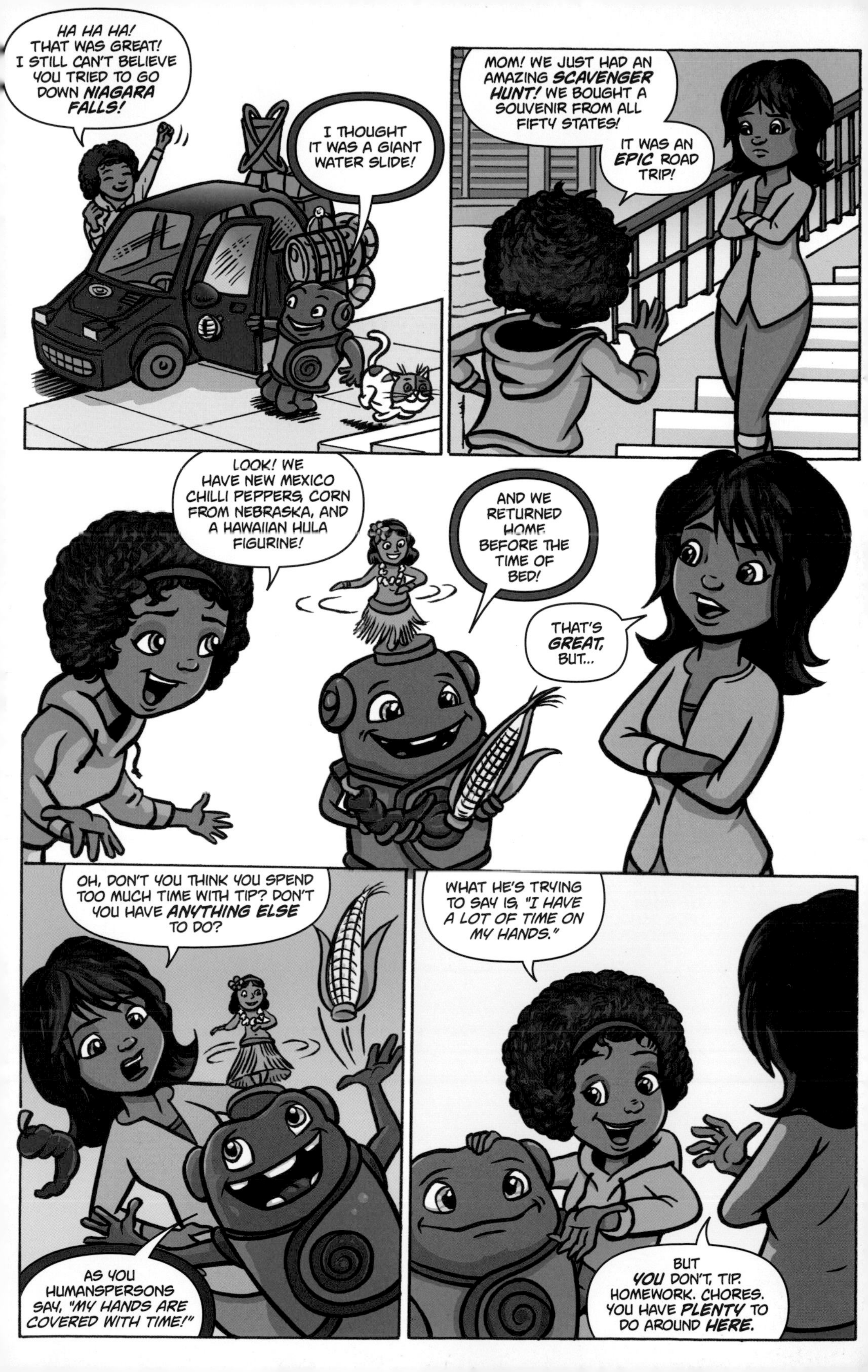

HA HA HA! THAT WAS GREAT! I STILL CAN'T BELIEVE YOU TRIED TO GO DOWN NIAGARA FALLS!
I THOUGHT IT WAS A GIANT WATER SLIDE!
MOM! WE JUST HAD AN AMAZING SCAVENGER HUNT! WE BOUGHT A SOUVENIR FROM ALL FIFTY STATES!
IT WAS AN EPIC ROAD TRIP!
LOOK! WE HAVE NEW MEXICO CHILLI PEPPERS, CORN FROM NEBRASKA, AND A HAWAIIAN HULA FIGURINE!
AND WE RETURNED HOME BEFORE THE TIME OF BED!
THAT'S GREAT, BUT...
OH, DON'T YOU THINK YOU SPEND TOO MUCH TIME WITH TIP? DON'T YOU HAVE ANYTHING ELSE TO DO?
AS YOU HUMANSPERSONS SAY, "MY HANDS ARE COVERED WITH TIME!"
WHAT HE'S TRYING TO SAY IS, "I HAVE A LOT OF TIME ON MY HANDS."
BUT YOU DON'T, TIP. HOMEWORK. CHORES. YOU HAVE PLENTY TO DO AROUND HERE.

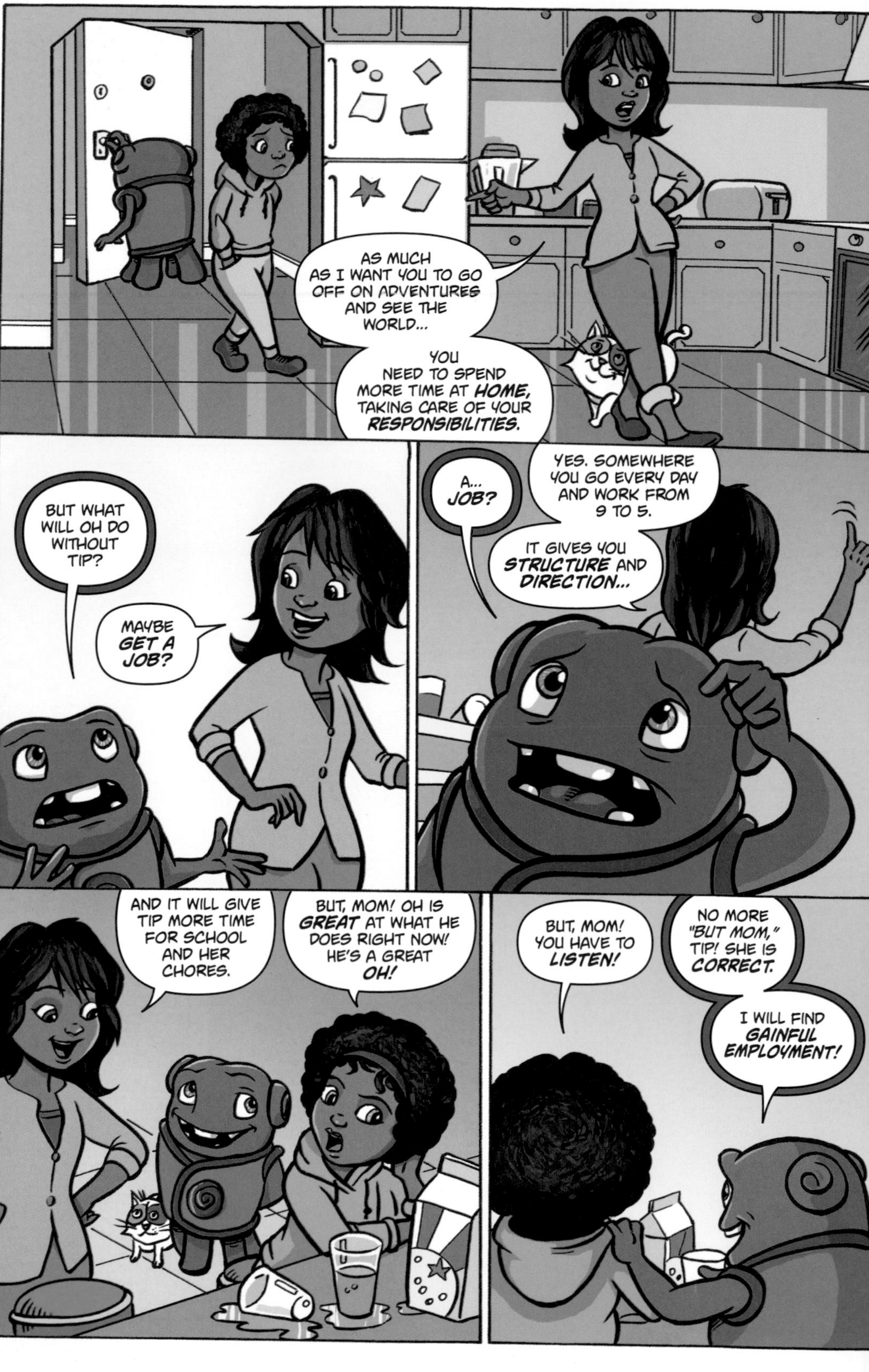
AS MUCH AS I WANT YOU TO GO OFF ON ADVENTURES AND SEE THE WORLD...
YOU NEED TO SPEND MORE TIME AT ***HOME,*** TAKING CARE OF YOUR ***RESPONSIBILITIES.***
BUT WHAT WILL OH DO WITHOUT TIP?
MAYBE ***GET A JOB?***
A... ***JOB?***
YES. SOMEWHERE YOU GO EVERY DAY AND WORK FROM 9 TO 5.
IT GIVES YOU ***STRUCTURE*** AND ***DIRECTION...***
AND IT WILL GIVE TIP MORE TIME FOR SCHOOL AND HER CHORES.
BUT, MOM! OH IS ***GREAT*** AT WHAT HE DOES RIGHT NOW! HE'S A GREAT ***OH!***
BUT, MOM! YOU HAVE TO ***LISTEN!***
NO MORE "BUT MOM," TIP! SHE IS ***CORRECT.***
I WILL FIND ***GAINFUL EMPLOYMENT!***

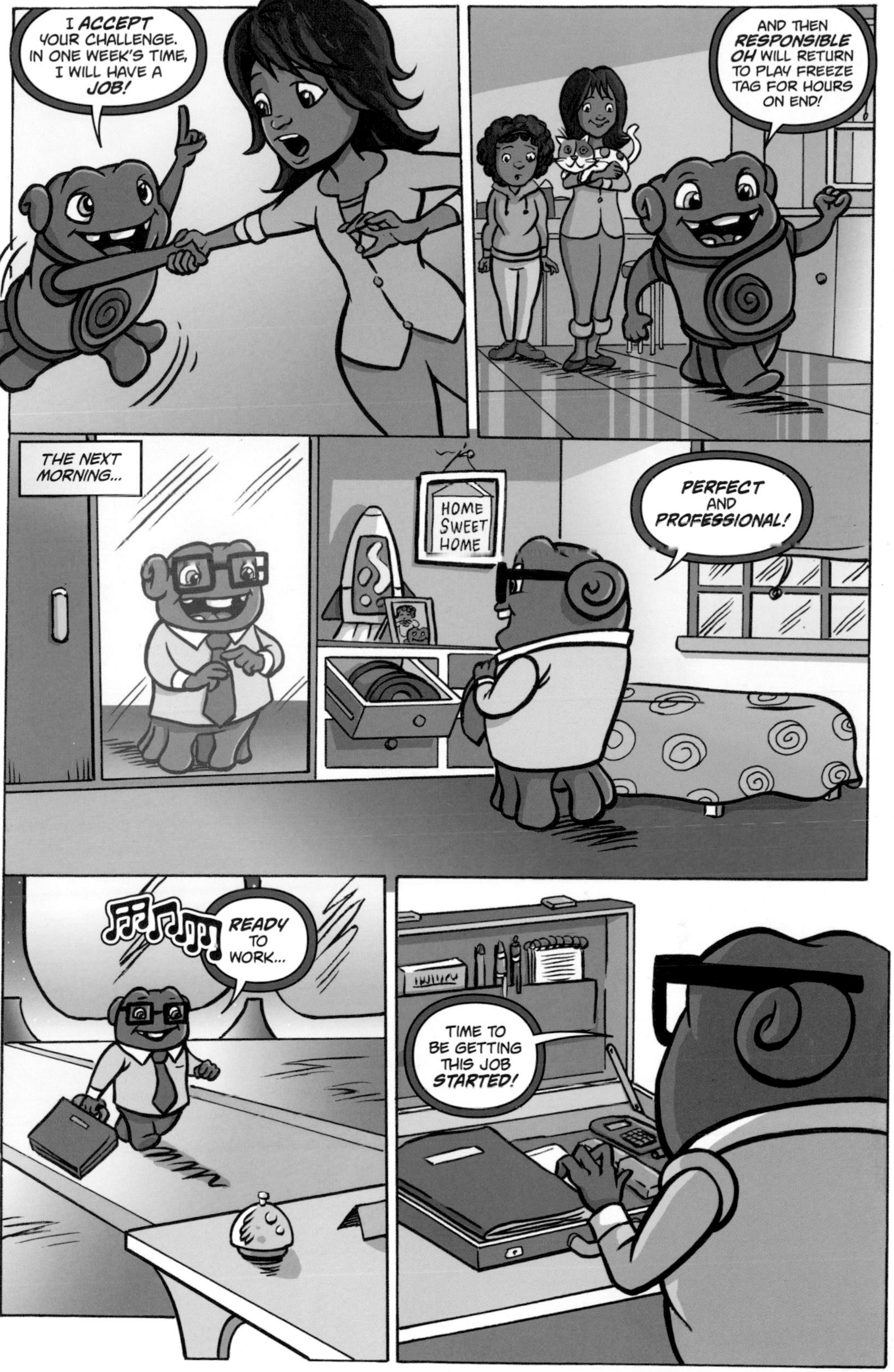
I ACCEPT YOUR CHALLENGE. IN ONE WEEK'S TIME, I WILL HAVE A JOB!
AND THEN RESPONSIBLE OH WILL RETURN TO PLAY FREEZE TAG FOR HOURS ON END!
THE NEXT MORNING...
HOME SWEET HOME
PERFECT AND PROFESSIONAL!
READY TO WORK...
TIME TO BE GETTING THIS JOB STARTED!

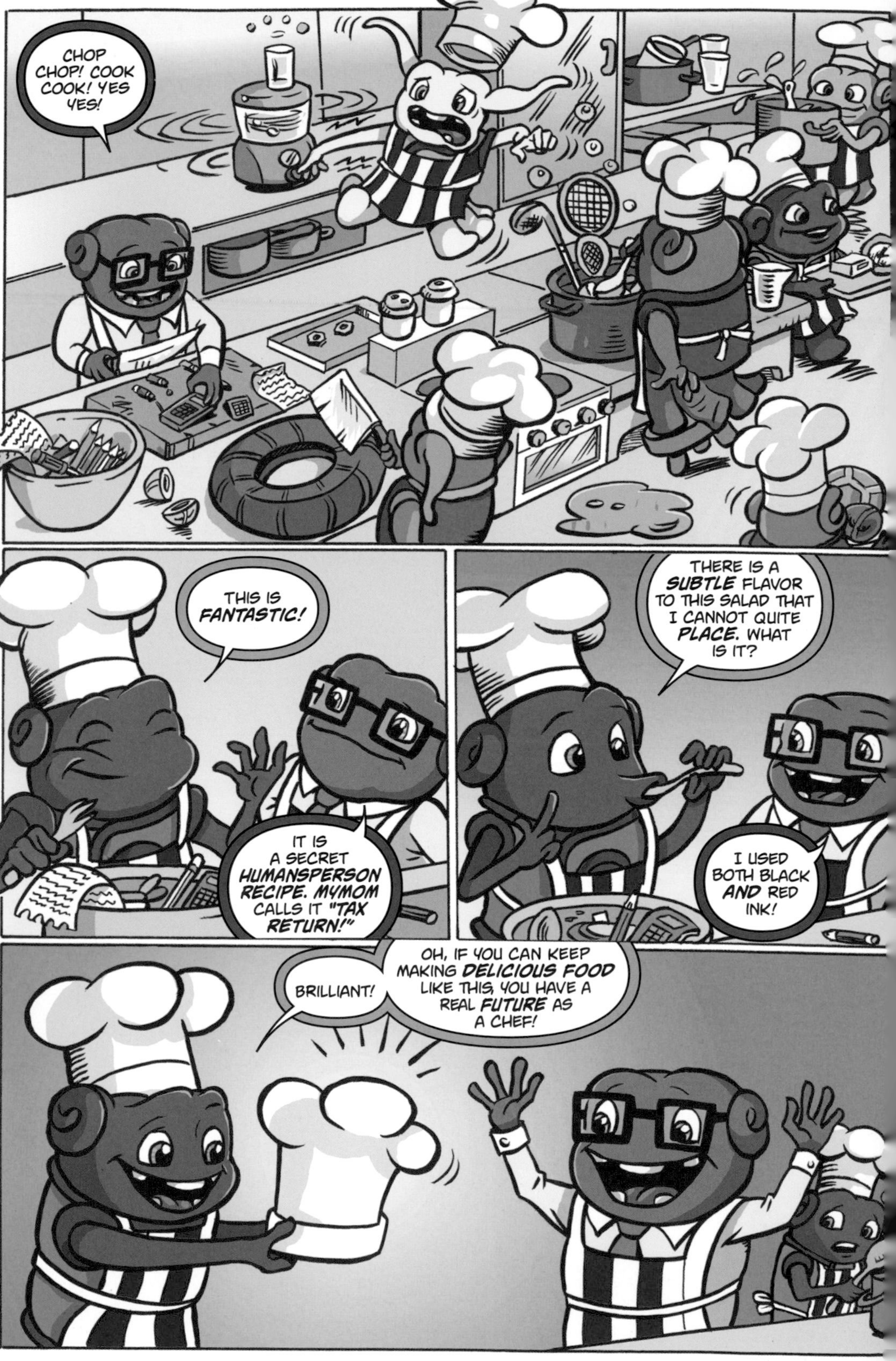
CHOP CHOP! COOK COOK! YES YES!
THIS IS FANTASTIC!
IT IS A SECRET HUMANSPERSON RECIPE. MYMOM CALLS IT "TAX RETURN!"
THERE IS A SUBTLE FLAVOR TO THIS SALAD THAT I CANNOT QUITE PLACE. WHAT IS IT?
I USED BOTH BLACK AND RED INK!
BRILLIANT!
OH, IF YOU CAN KEEP MAKING DELICIOUS FOOD LIKE THIS, YOU HAVE A REAL FUTURE AS A CHEF!

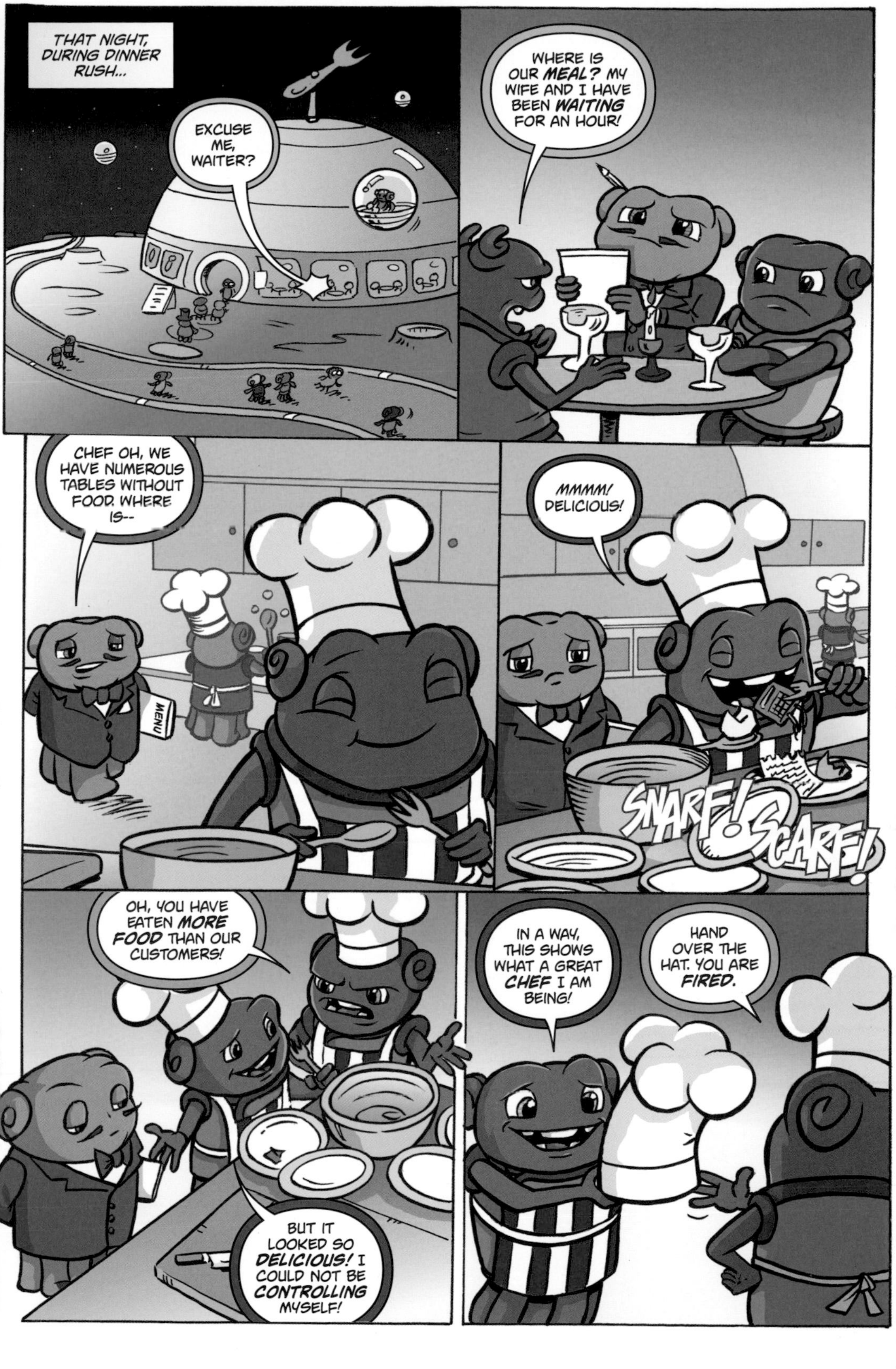
THAT NIGHT, DURING DINNER RUSH...
EXCUSE ME, WAITER?
WHERE IS OUR MEAL? MY WIFE AND I HAVE BEEN WAITING FOR AN HOUR!
CHEF OH, WE HAVE NUMEROUS TABLES WITHOUT FOOD. WHERE IS--
MENU
MMMM! DELICIOUS!
SNARF! SCARF!
OH, YOU HAVE EATEN MORE FOOD THAN OUR CUSTOMERS!
BUT IT LOOKED SO DELICIOUS! I COULD NOT BE CONTROLLING MYSELF!
IN A WAY, THIS SHOWS WHAT A GREAT CHEF I AM BEING!
HAND OVER THE HAT. YOU ARE FIRED.

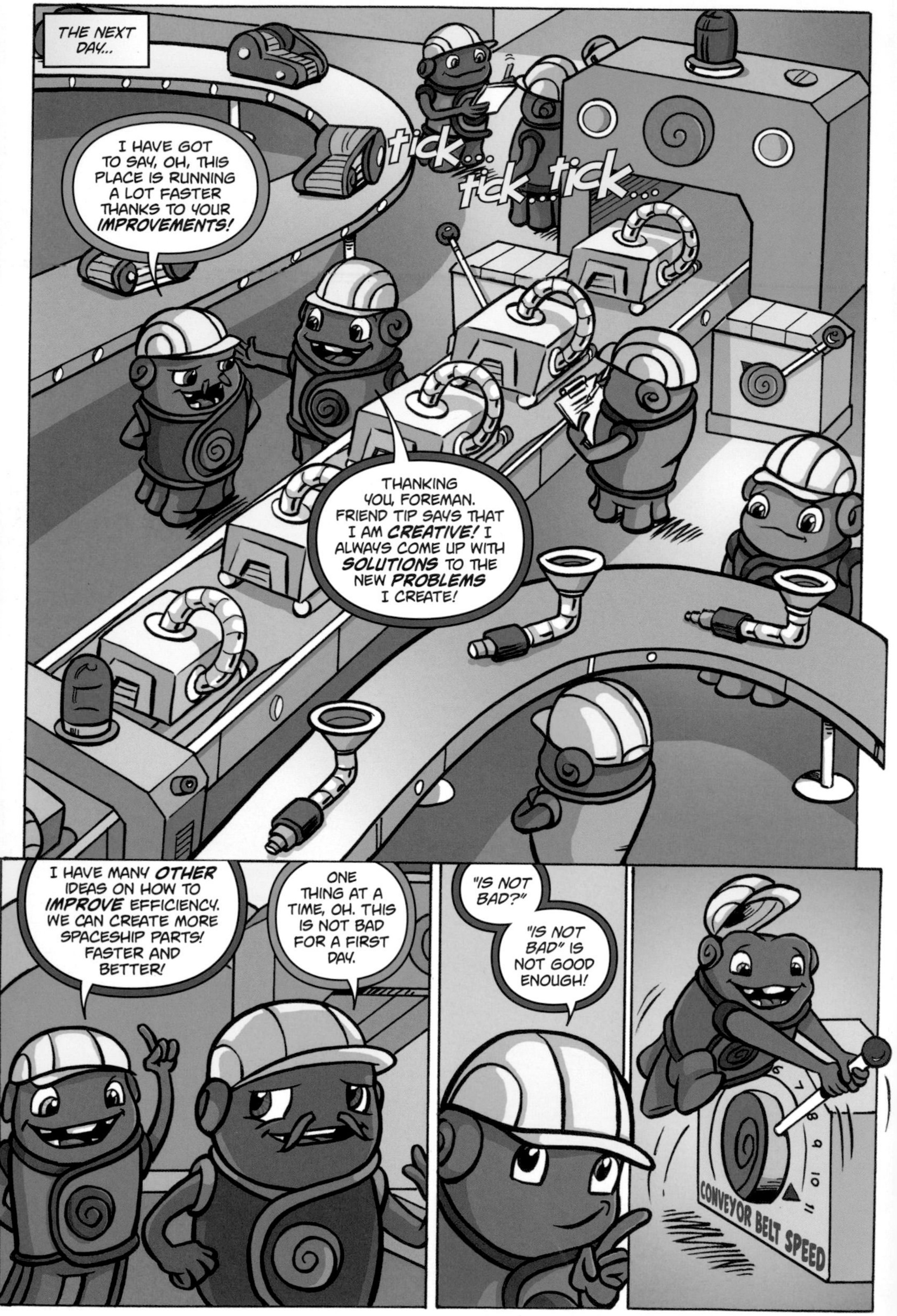
THE NEXT DAY...
I HAVE GOT TO SAY, OH, THIS PLACE IS RUNNING A LOT FASTER THANKS TO YOUR IMPROVEMENTS!
tick... tick tick...
THANKING YOU, FOREMAN. FRIEND TIP SAYS THAT I AM CREATIVE! I ALWAYS COME UP WITH SOLUTIONS TO THE NEW PROBLEMS I CREATE!
I HAVE MANY OTHER IDEAS ON HOW TO IMPROVE EFFICIENCY. WE CAN CREATE MORE SPACESHIP PARTS! FASTER AND BETTER!
ONE THING AT A TIME, OH. THIS IS NOT BAD FOR A FIRST DAY.
"IS NOT BAD?"
"IS NOT BAD" IS NOT GOOD ENOUGH!
CONVEYOR BELT SPEED

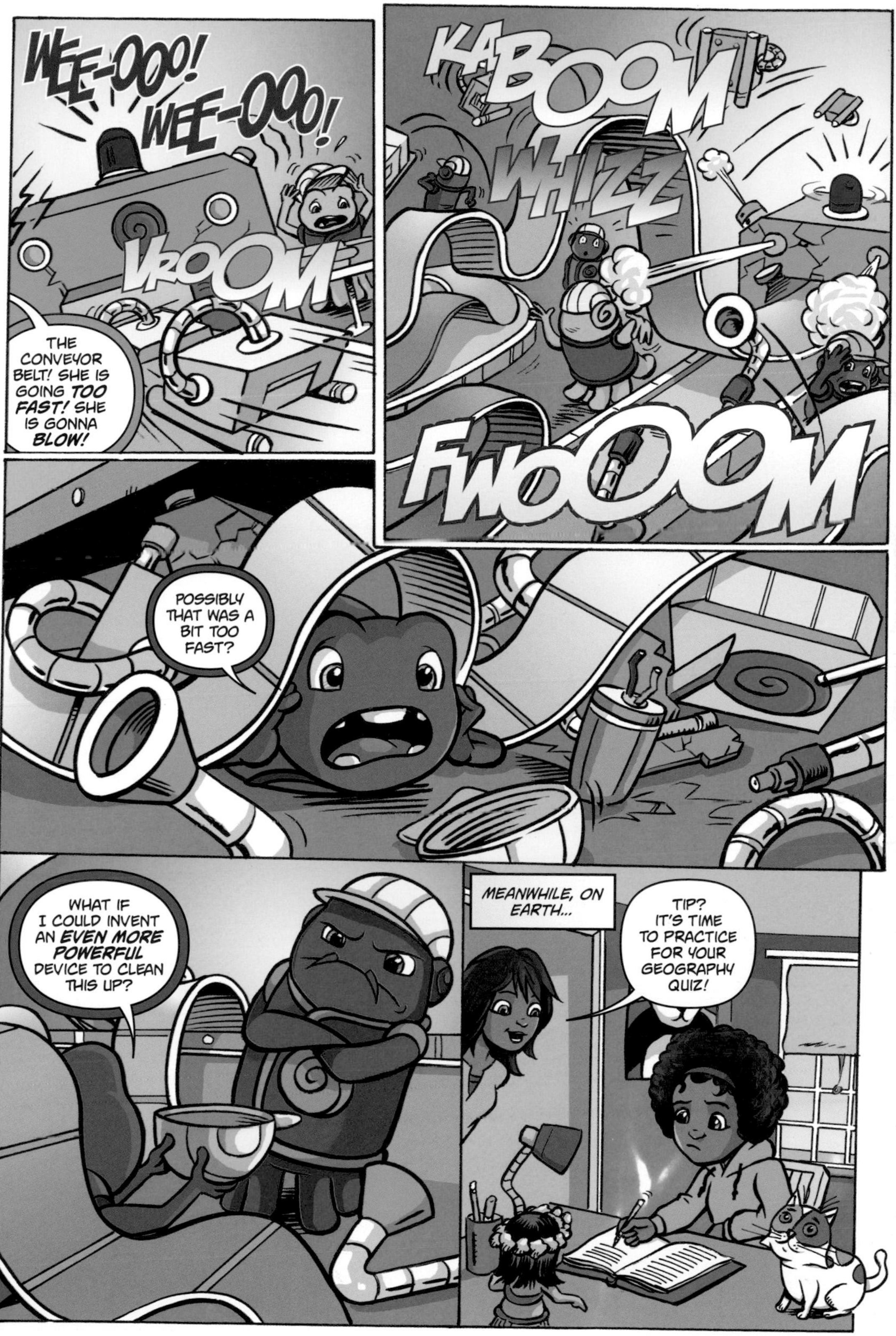
WEE-OOO! WEE-OOO!
VROOM
THE CONVEYOR BELT! SHE IS GOING TOO FAST! SHE IS GONNA BLOW!
KABOOM
WHIZZ
FWOOOM
POSSIBLY THAT WAS A BIT TOO FAST?
WHAT IF I COULD INVENT AN EVEN MORE POWERFUL DEVICE TO CLEAN THIS UP?
MEANWHILE, ON EARTH...
TIP? IT'S TIME TO PRACTICE FOR YOUR GEOGRAPHY QUIZ!

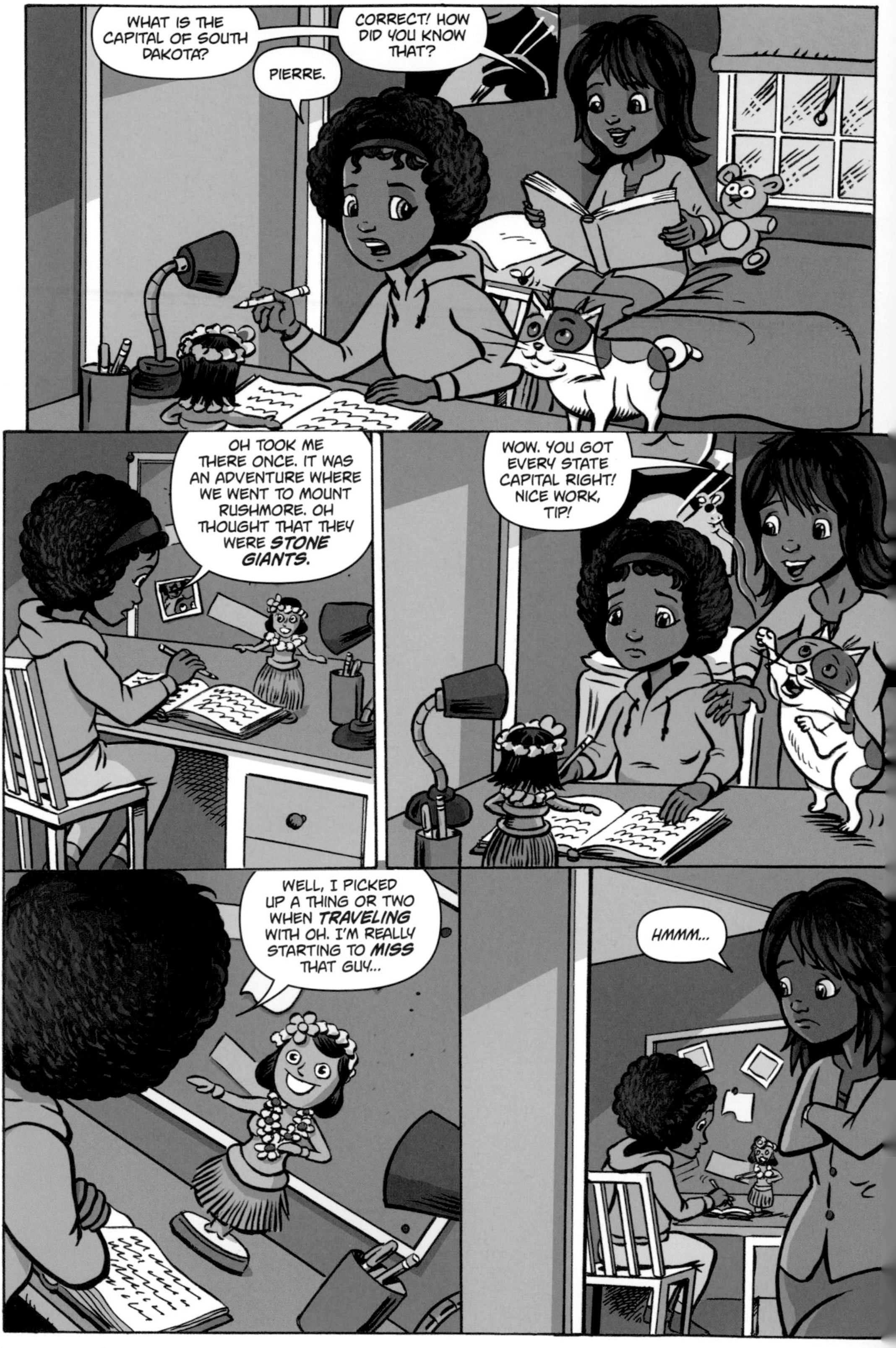
WHAT IS THE CAPITAL OF SOUTH DAKOTA?
PIERRE.
CORRECT! HOW DID YOU KNOW THAT?
OH TOOK ME THERE ONCE. IT WAS AN ADVENTURE WHERE WE WENT TO MOUNT RUSHMORE. OH THOUGHT THAT THEY WERE STONE GIANTS.
WOW. YOU GOT EVERY STATE CAPITAL RIGHT! NICE WORK, TIP!
WELL, I PICKED UP A THING OR TWO WHEN TRAVELING WITH OH. I'M REALLY STARTING TO MISS THAT GUY...
HMMM...

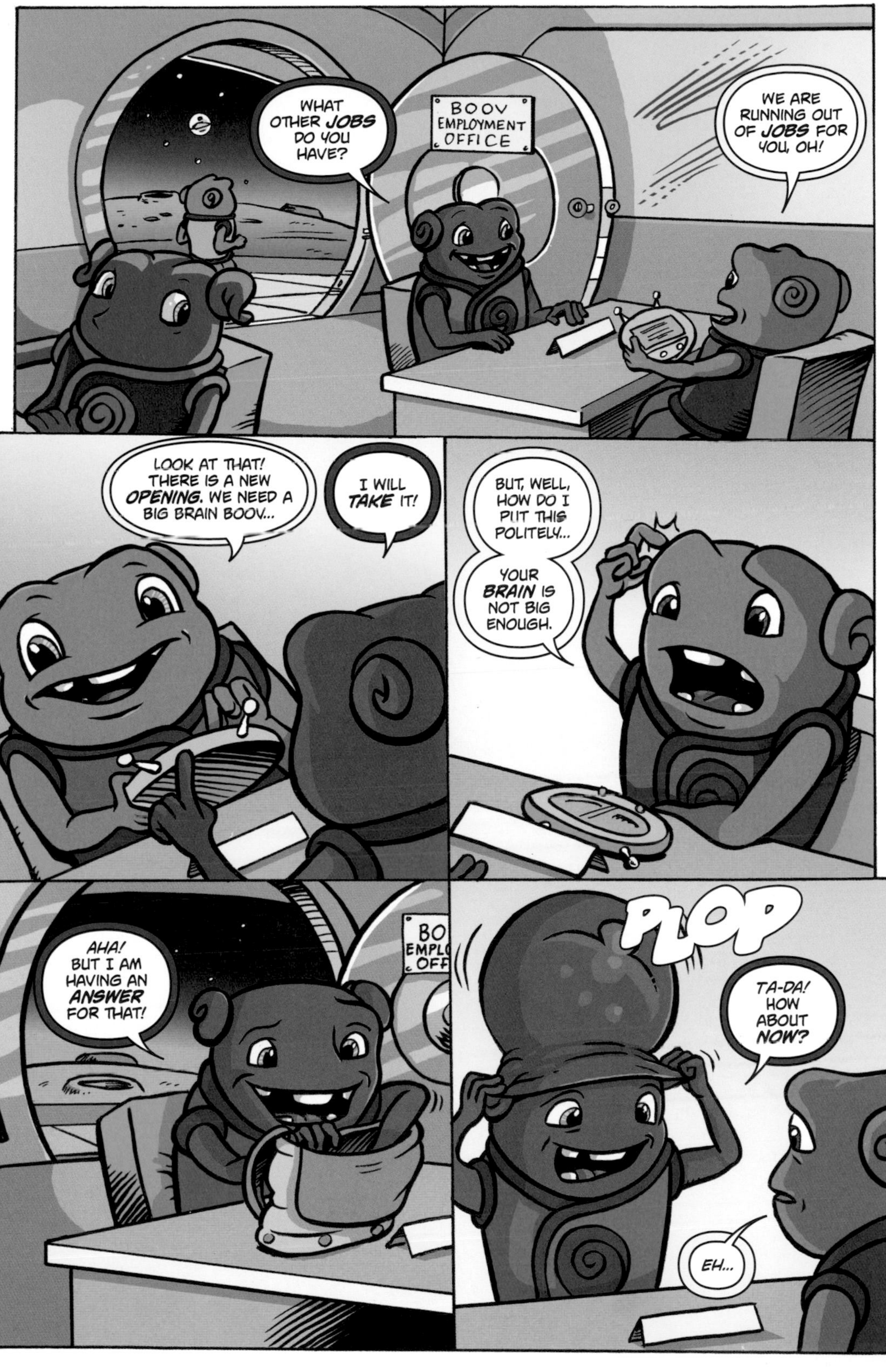

WHAT OTHER JOBS DO YOU HAVE?
BOOV EMPLOYMENT OFFICE
WE ARE RUNNING OUT OF JOBS FOR YOU, OH!
LOOK AT THAT! THERE IS A NEW OPENING. WE NEED A BIG BRAIN BOOV...
I WILL TAKE IT!
BUT, WELL, HOW DO I PUT THIS POLITELY...
YOUR BRAIN IS NOT BIG ENOUGH.
AHA! BUT I AM HAVING AN ANSWER FOR THAT!
PLOP
TA-DA! HOW ABOUT NOW?
EH...

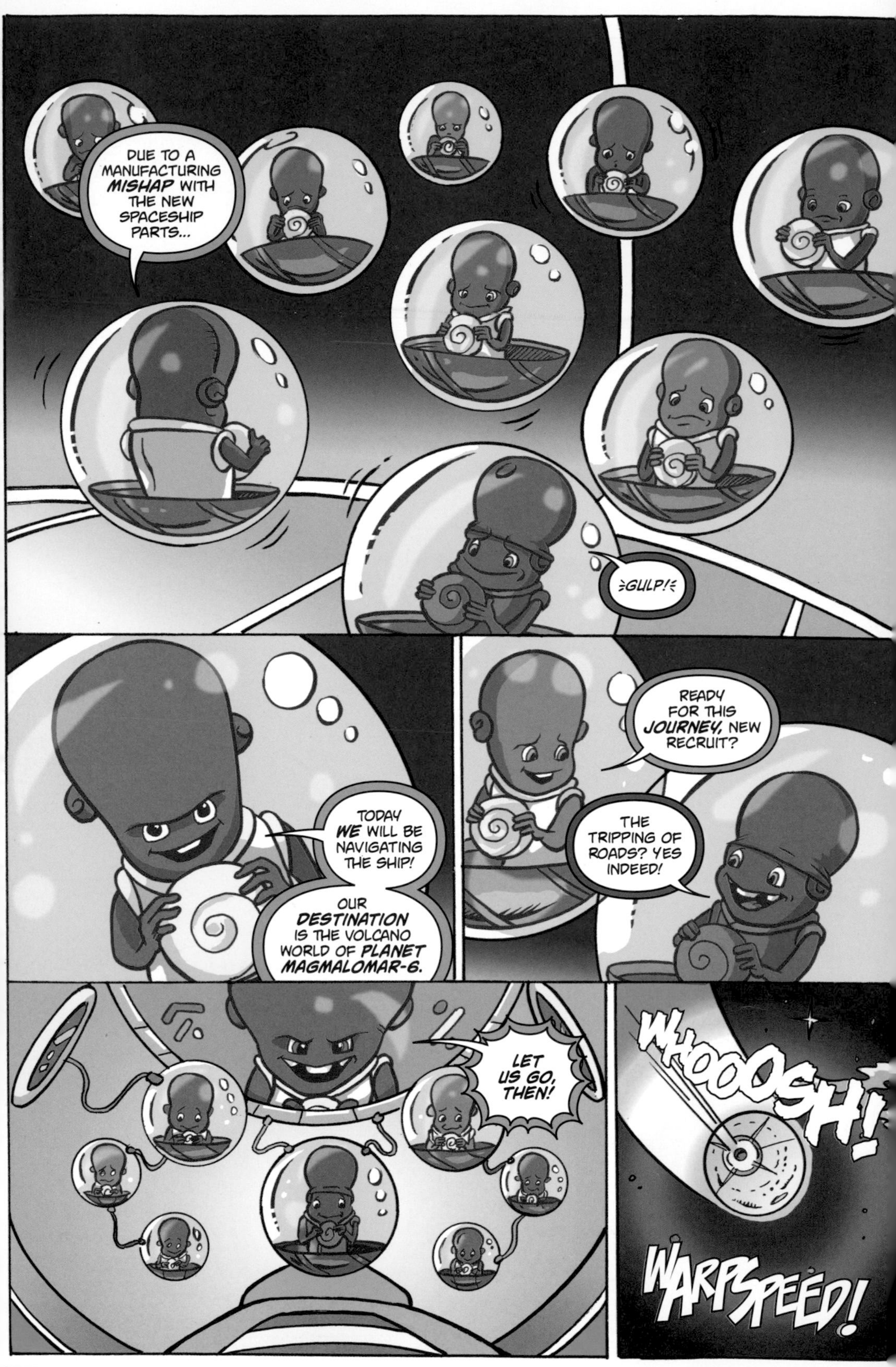
DUE TO A MANUFACTURING MISHAP WITH THE NEW SPACESHIP PARTS...
GULP!
TODAY WE WILL BE NAVIGATING THE SHIP!
OUR DESTINATION IS THE VOLCANO WORLD OF PLANET MAGMALOMAR-6.
READY FOR THIS JOURNEY, NEW RECRUIT?
THE TRIPPING OF ROADS? YES INDEED!
LET US GO, THEN!
WHOOOSH!
WARP SPEED!

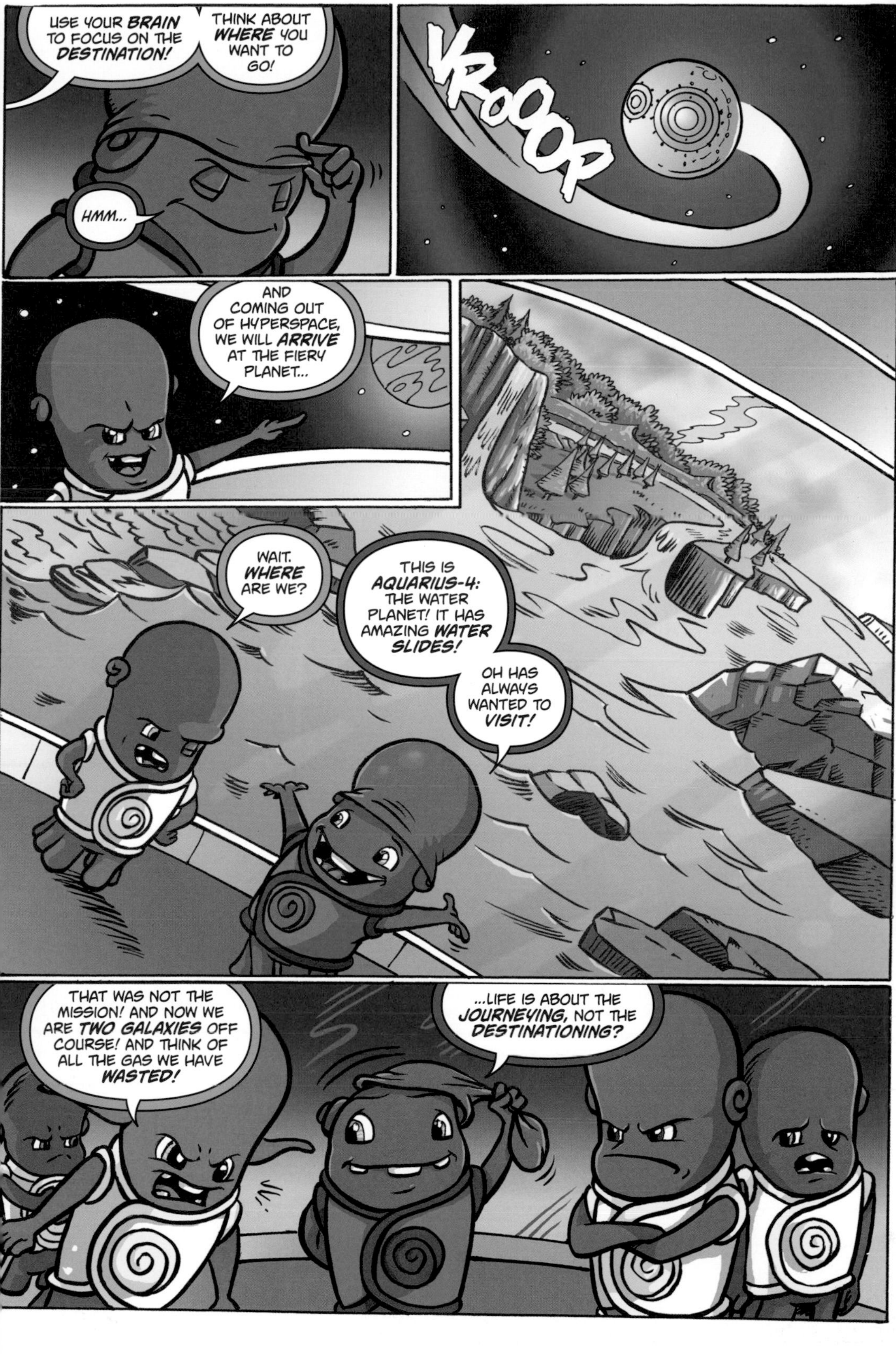
USE YOUR BRAIN TO FOCUS ON THE DESTINATION!
THINK ABOUT WHERE YOU WANT TO GO!
HMM...
VROOOOP
AND COMING OUT OF HYPERSPACE, WE WILL ARRIVE AT THE FIERY PLANET...
WAIT. WHERE ARE WE?
THIS IS AQUARIUS-4: THE WATER PLANET! IT HAS AMAZING WATER SLIDES!
OH HAS ALWAYS WANTED TO VISIT!
THAT WAS NOT THE MISSION! AND NOW WE ARE TWO GALAXIES OFF COURSE! AND THINK OF ALL THE GAS WE HAVE WASTED!
...LIFE IS ABOUT THE JOURNEYING, NOT THE DESTINATIONING?

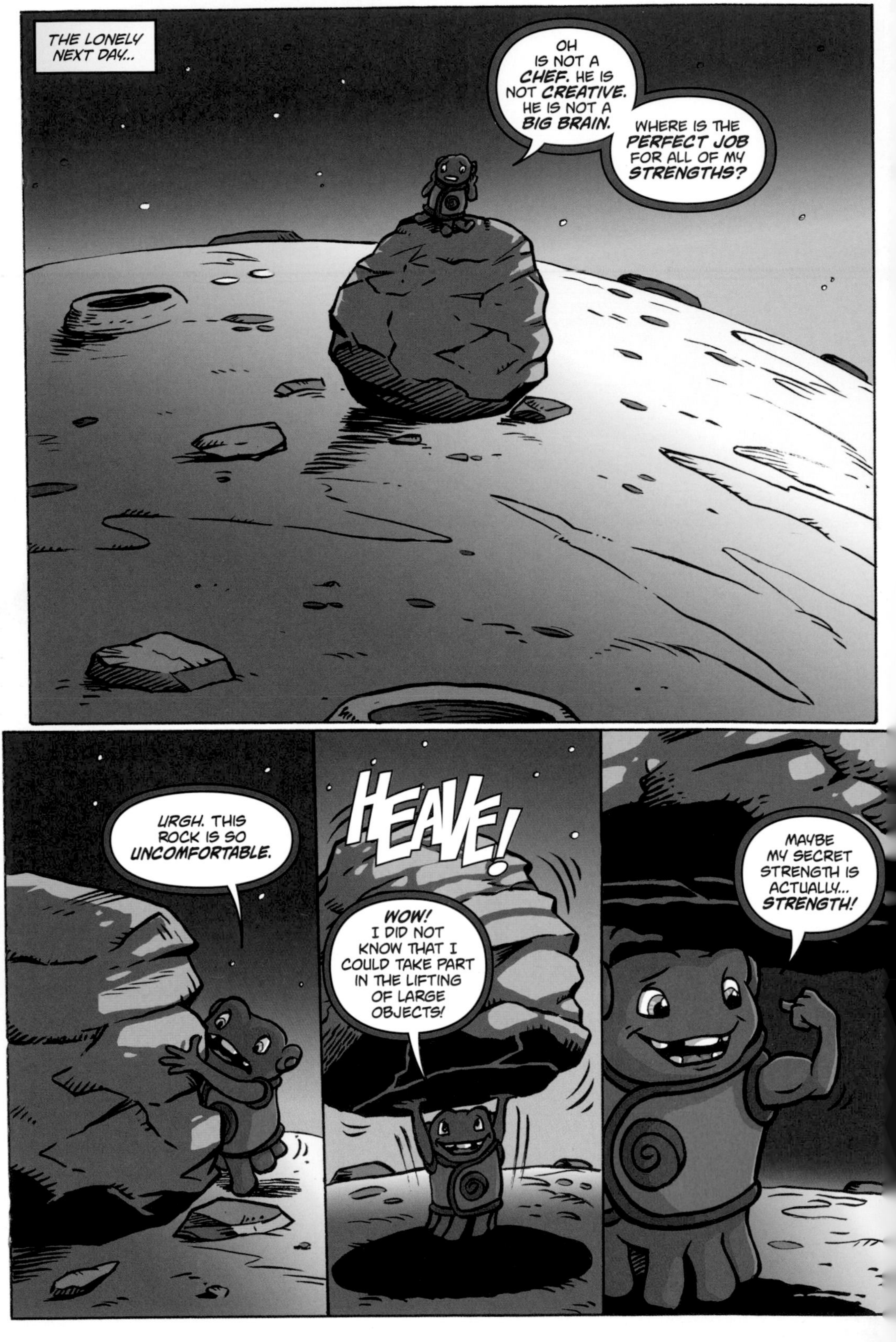

THE LONELY NEXT DAY...
OH IS NOT A CHEF. HE IS NOT CREATIVE. HE IS NOT A BIG BRAIN.
WHERE IS THE PERFECT JOB FOR ALL OF MY STRENGTHS?
URGH. THIS ROCK IS SO UNCOMFORTABLE.
HEAVE!
WOW! I DID NOT KNOW THAT I COULD TAKE PART IN THE LIFTING OF LARGE OBJECTS!
MAYBE MY SECRET STRENGTH IS ACTUALLY... STRENGTH!

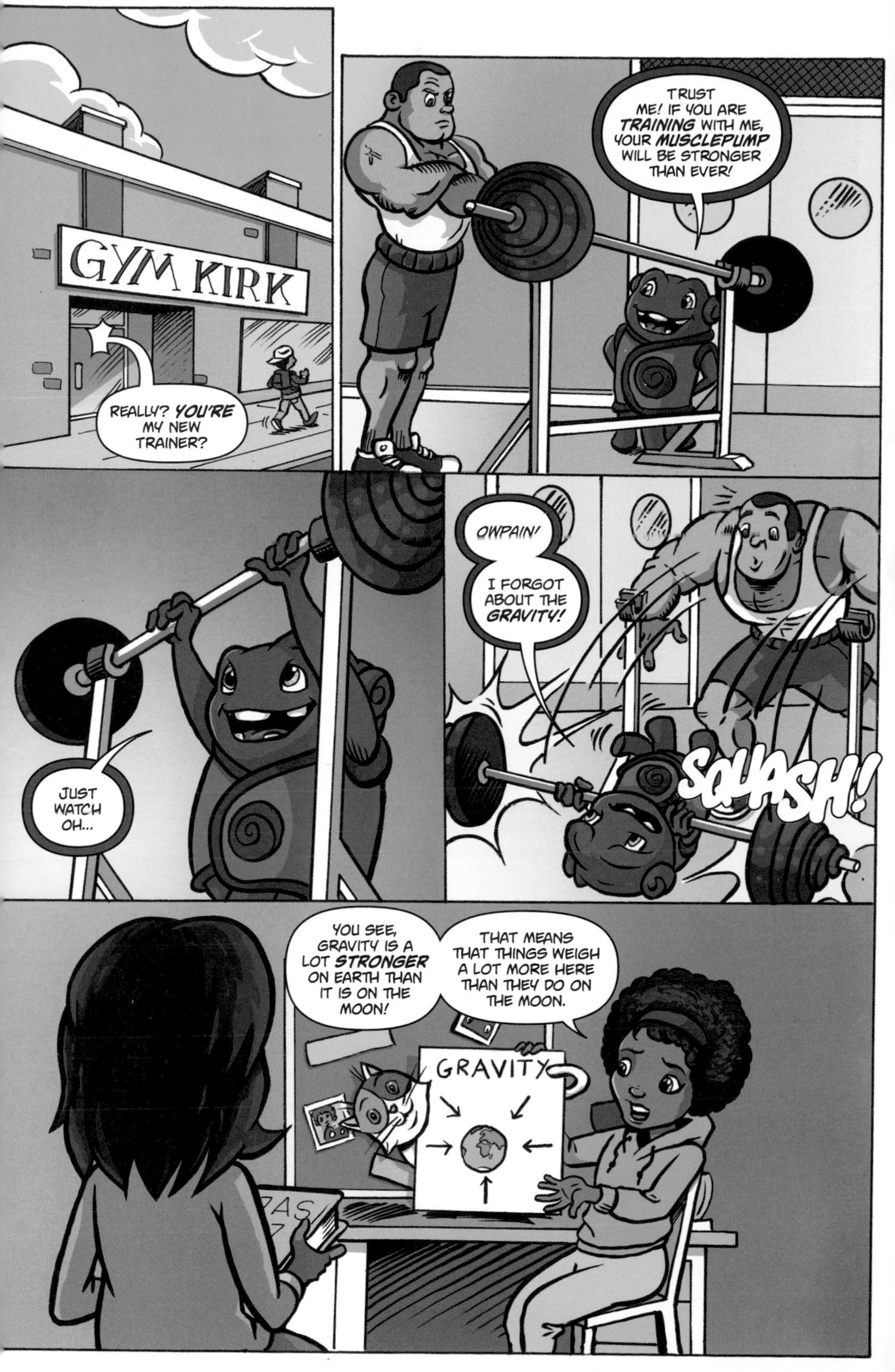
GYM KIRK
REALLY? YOU'RE MY NEW TRAINER?
TRUST ME! IF YOU ARE TRAINING WITH ME, YOUR MUSCLEPUMP WILL BE STRONGER THAN EVER!
JUST WATCH OH...
OWPAIN!
I FORGOT ABOUT THE GRAVITY!
SQUASH!
YOU SEE, GRAVITY IS A LOT STRONGER ON EARTH THAN IT IS ON THE MOON!
THAT MEANS THAT THINGS WEIGH A LOT MORE HERE THAN THEY DO ON THE MOON.
GRAVITY

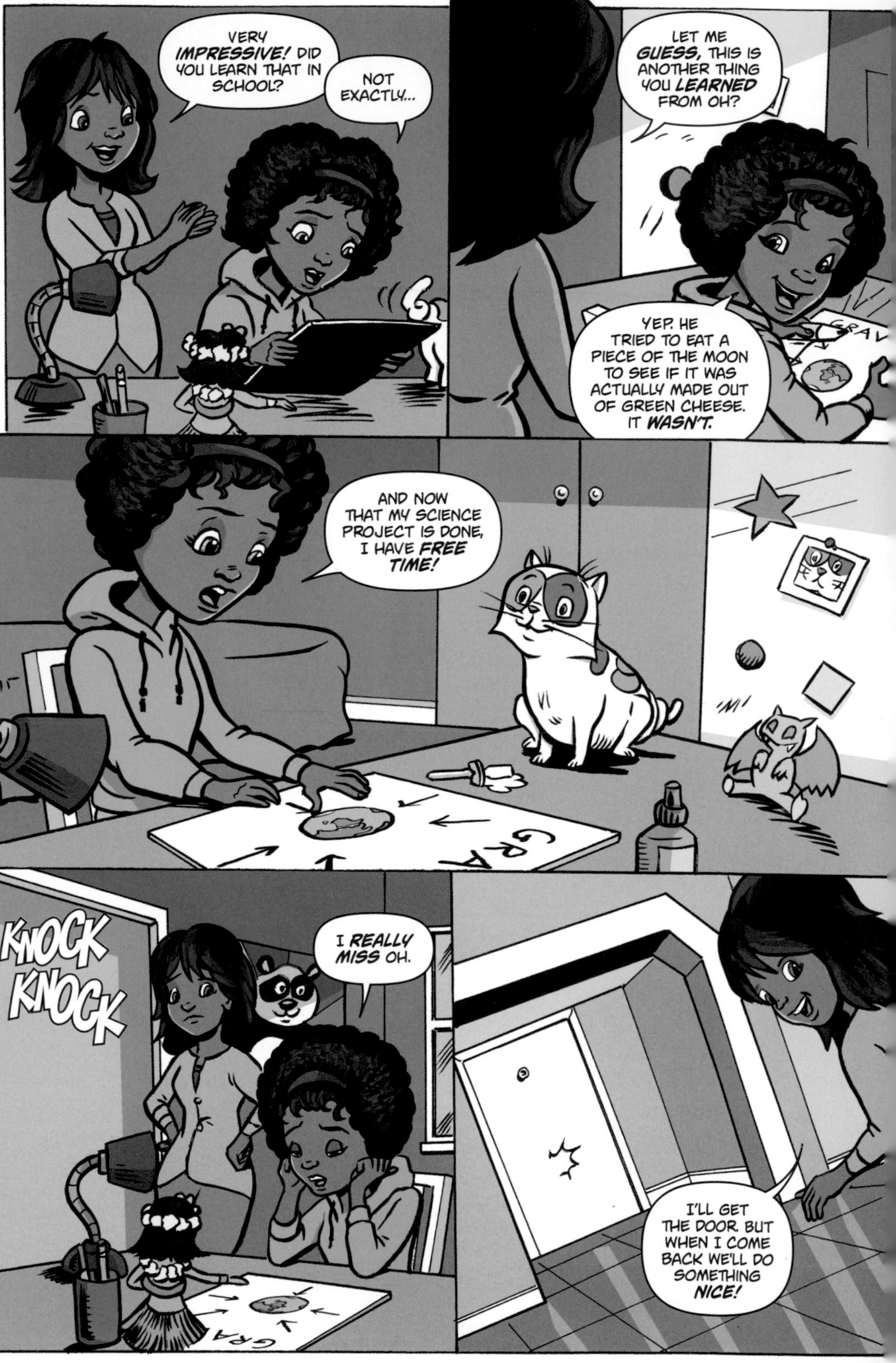
VERY IMPRESSIVE! DID YOU LEARN THAT IN SCHOOL?
NOT EXACTLY...
LET ME GUESS, THIS IS ANOTHER THING YOU LEARNED FROM OH?
YEP. HE TRIED TO EAT A PIECE OF THE MOON TO SEE IF IT WAS ACTUALLY MADE OUT OF GREEN CHEESE. IT WASN'T.
AND NOW THAT MY SCIENCE PROJECT IS DONE, I HAVE FREE TIME!
KNOCK KNOCK
I REALLY MISS OH.
I'LL GET THE DOOR. BUT WHEN I COME BACK WE'LL DO SOMETHING NICE!

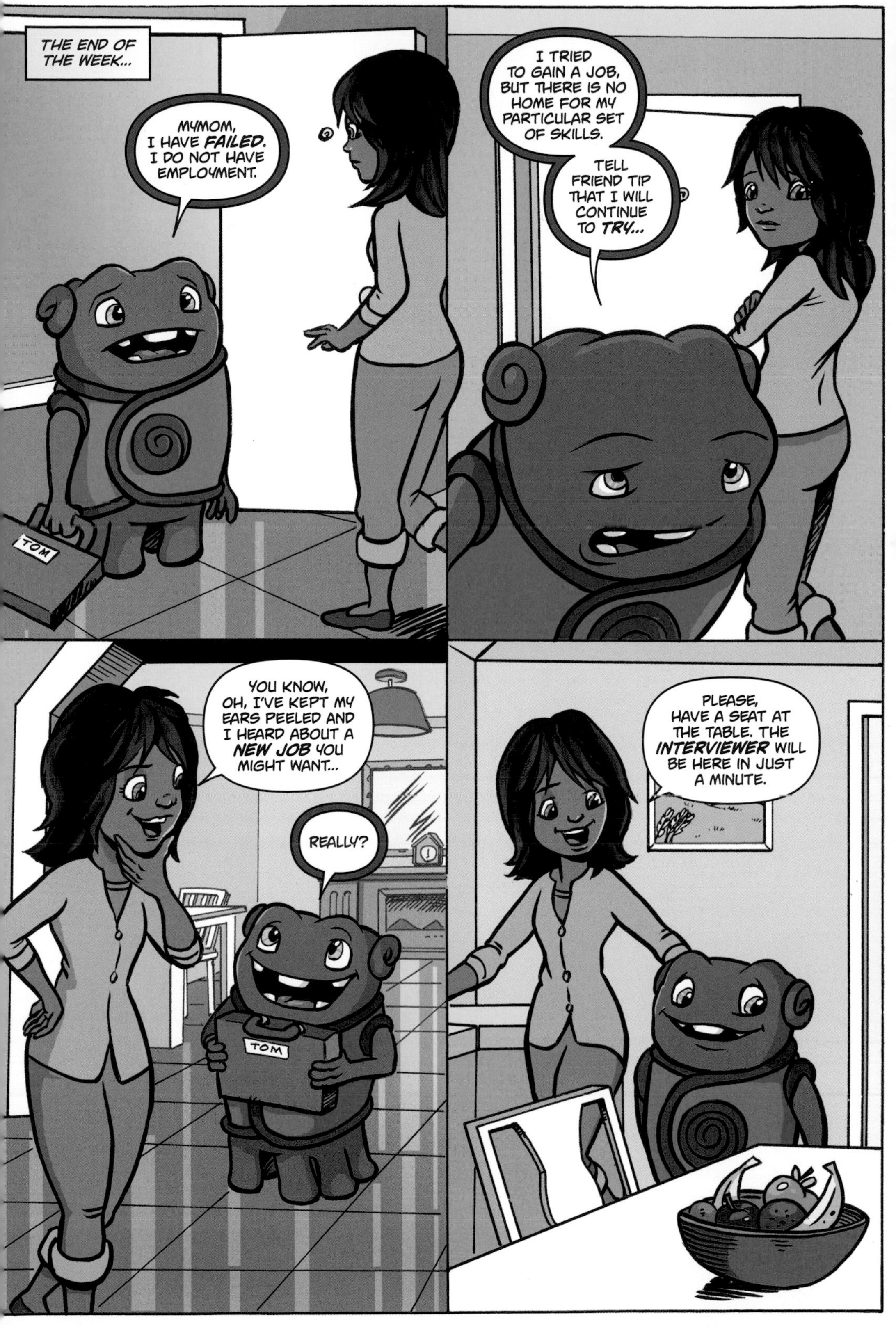
THE END OF THE WEEK...
MYMOM, I HAVE FAILED. I DO NOT HAVE EMPLOYMENT.
I TRIED TO GAIN A JOB, BUT THERE IS NO HOME FOR MY PARTICULAR SET OF SKILLS.
TELL FRIEND TIP THAT I WILL CONTINUE TO TRY...
TOM
YOU KNOW, OH, I'VE KEPT MY EARS PEELED AND I HEARD ABOUT A NEW JOB YOU MIGHT WANT...
REALLY?
TOM
PLEASE, HAVE A SEAT AT THE TABLE. THE INTERVIEWER WILL BE HERE IN JUST A MINUTE.

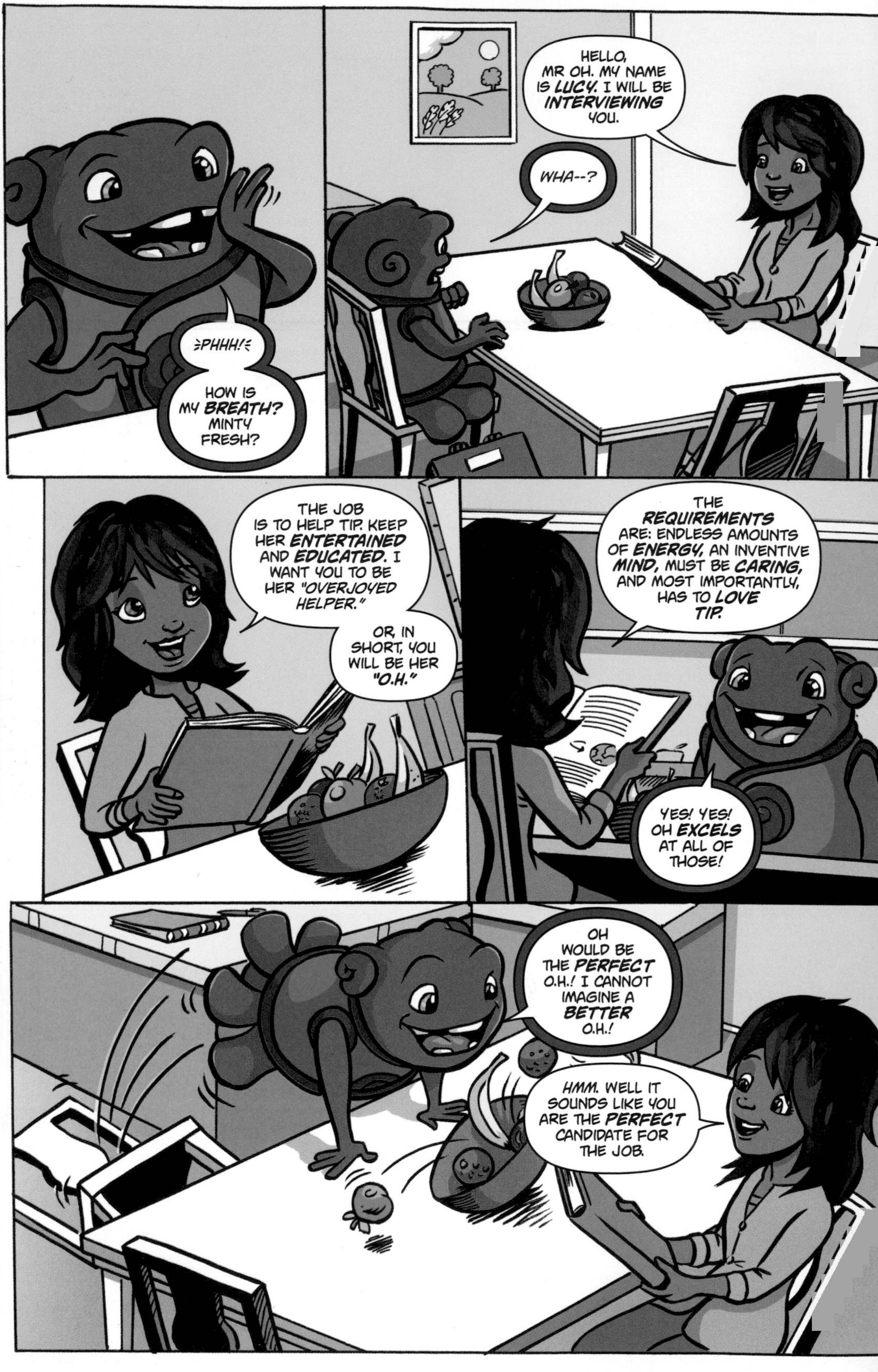

≥PHHH!≤
HOW IS MY BREATH? MINTY FRESH?
HELLO, MR OH. MY NAME IS LUCY. I WILL BE INTERVIEWING YOU.
WHA--?
THE JOB IS TO HELP TIP. KEEP HER ENTERTAINED AND EDUCATED. I WANT YOU TO BE HER "OVERJOYED HELPER."
OR, IN SHORT, YOU WILL BE HER "O.H."
THE REQUIREMENTS ARE: ENDLESS AMOUNTS OF ENERGY, AN INVENTIVE MIND, MUST BE CARING, AND MOST IMPORTANTLY, HAS TO LOVE TIP.
YES! YES! OH EXCELS AT ALL OF THOSE!
OH WOULD BE THE PERFECT O.H.! I CANNOT IMAGINE A BETTER O.H.!
HMM. WELL IT SOUNDS LIKE YOU ARE THE PERFECT CANDIDATE FOR THE JOB.

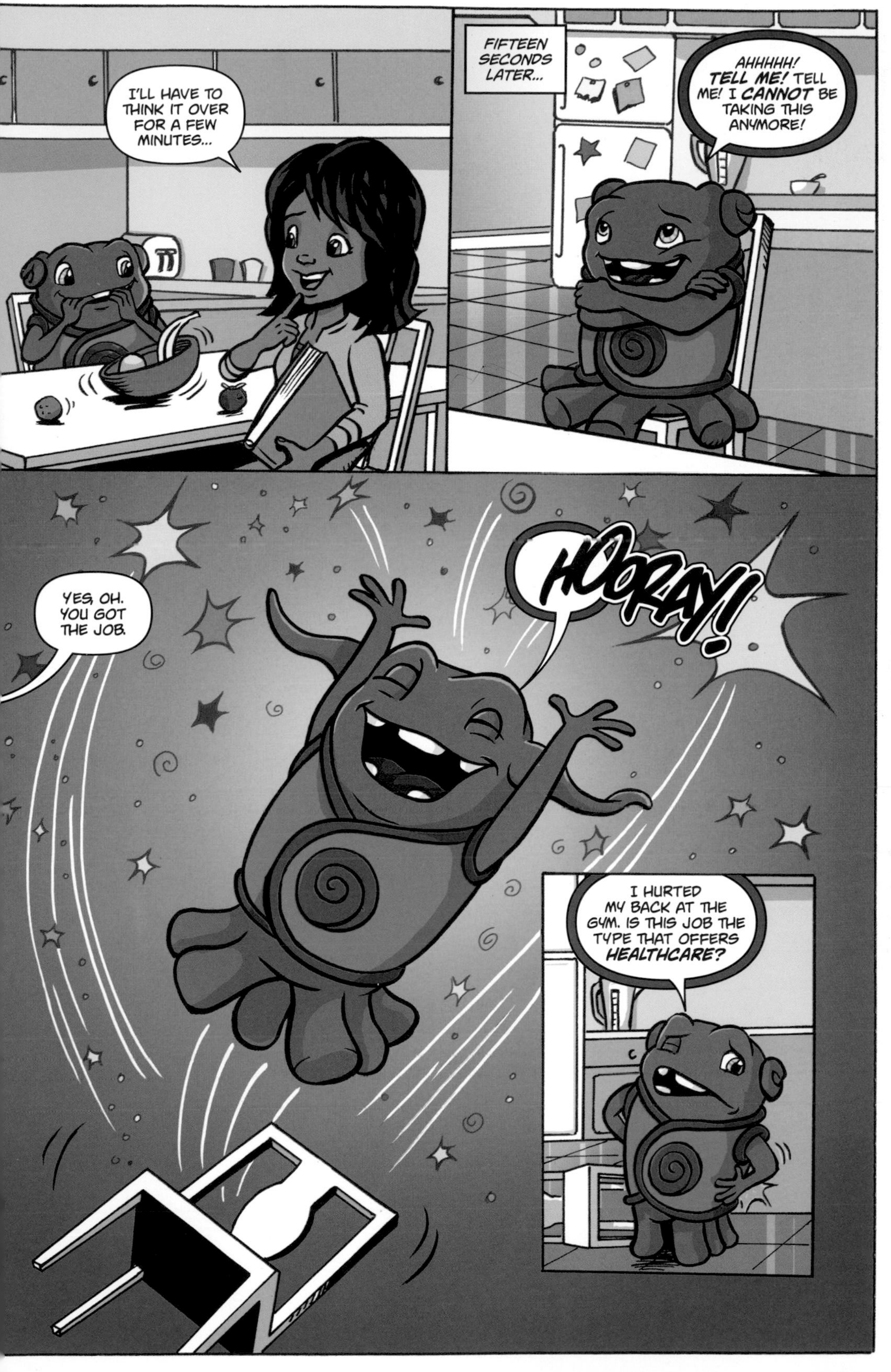
I'LL HAVE TO THINK IT OVER FOR A FEW MINUTES...
FIFTEEN SECONDS LATER...
AHHHHH! TELL ME! TELL ME! I CANNOT BE TAKING THIS ANYMORE!
YES, OH. YOU GOT THE JOB.
HOORAY!
I HURTED MY BACK AT THE GYM. IS THIS JOB THE TYPE THAT OFFERS HEALTHCARE?

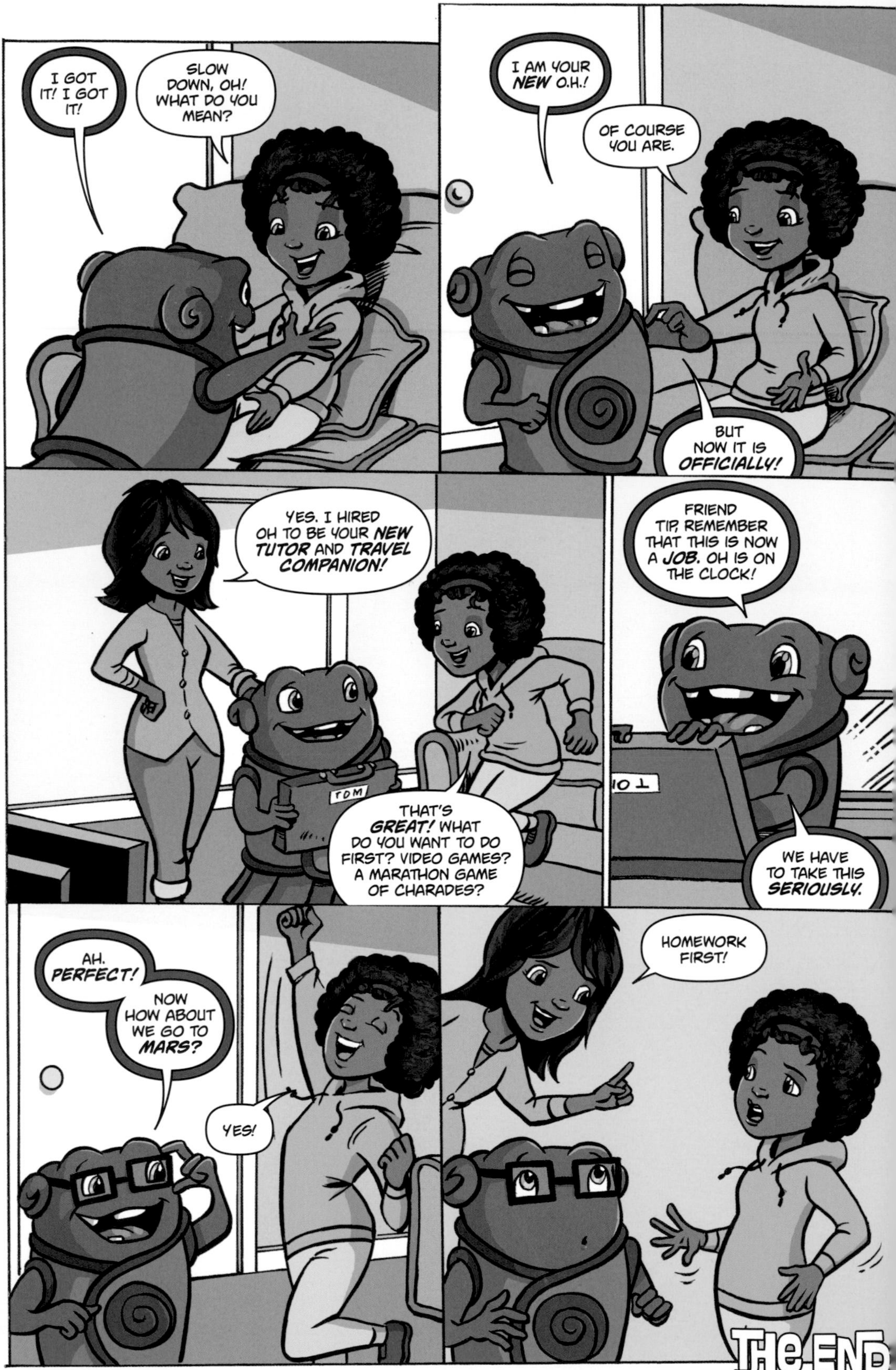
I GOT IT! I GOT IT!
SLOW DOWN, OH! WHAT DO YOU MEAN?
I AM YOUR NEW O.H.!
OF COURSE YOU ARE.
BUT NOW IT IS OFFICIALLY!
YES. I HIRED OH TO BE YOUR NEW TUTOR AND TRAVEL COMPANION!
TOM
THAT'S GREAT! WHAT DO YOU WANT TO DO FIRST? VIDEO GAMES? A MARATHON GAME OF CHARADES?
FRIEND TIP, REMEMBER THAT THIS IS NOW A JOB. OH IS ON THE CLOCK!
WE HAVE TO TAKE THIS SERIOUSLY.
AH. PERFECT!
NOW HOW ABOUT WE GO TO MARS?
YES!
HOMEWORK FIRST!
THE END

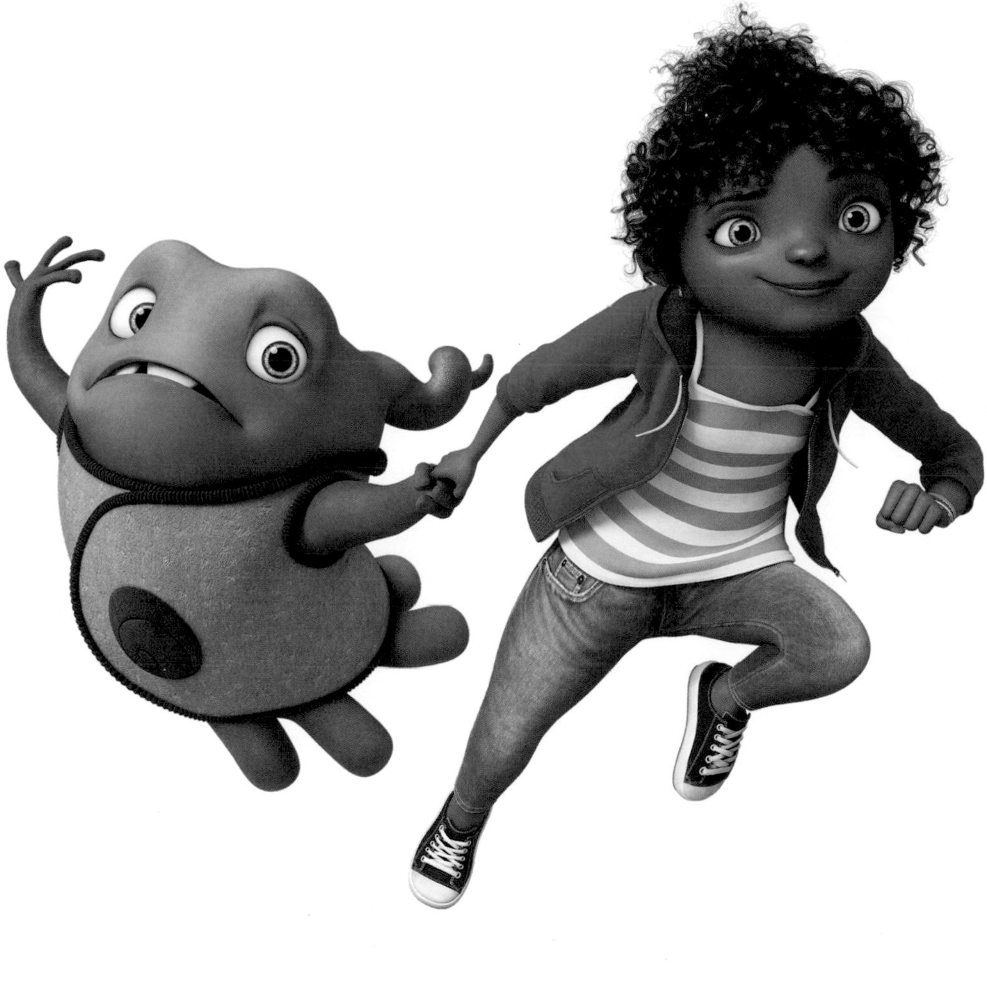

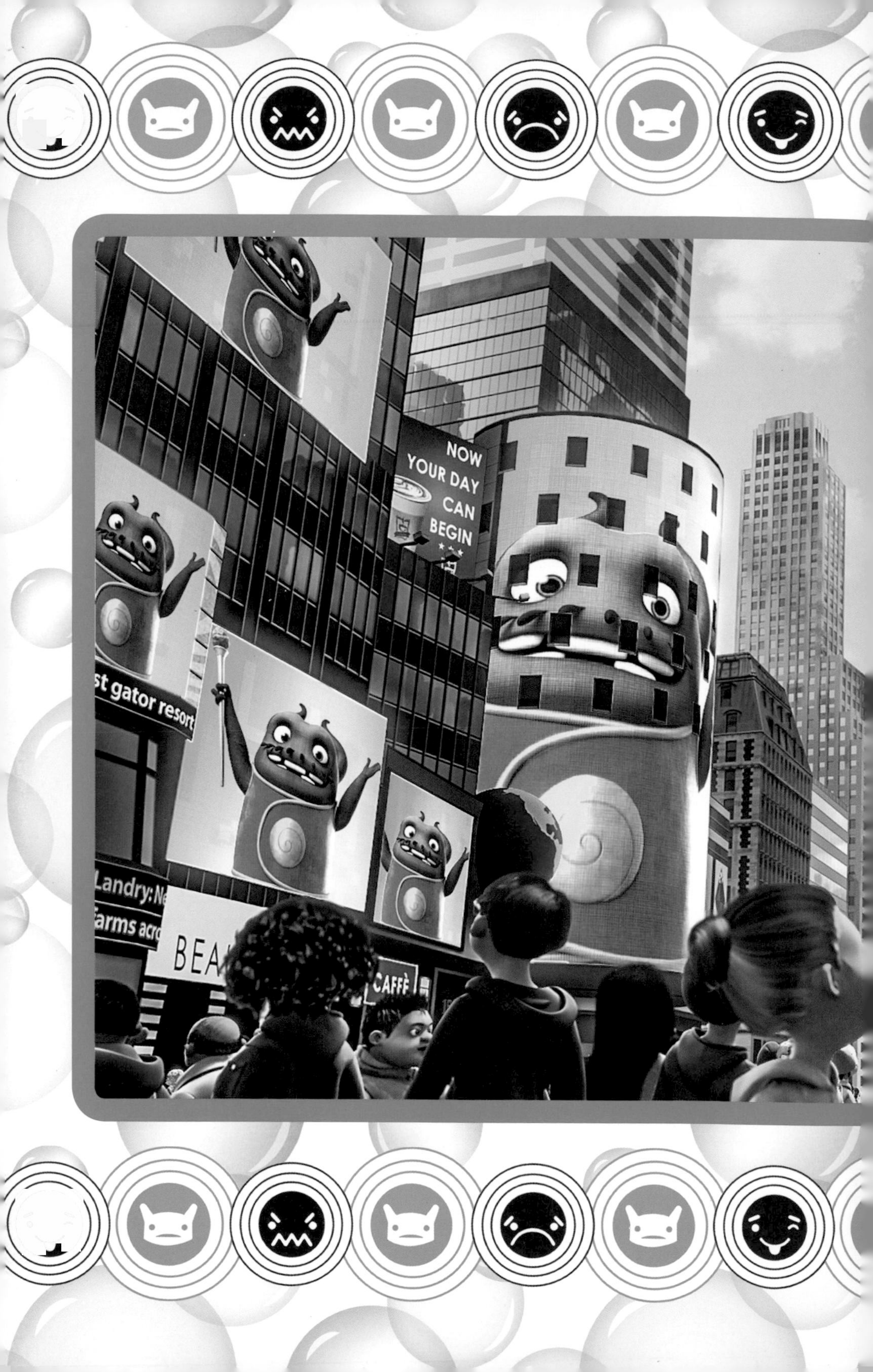
NOW
YOUR DAY
CAN
BEGIN
CAFFÈ

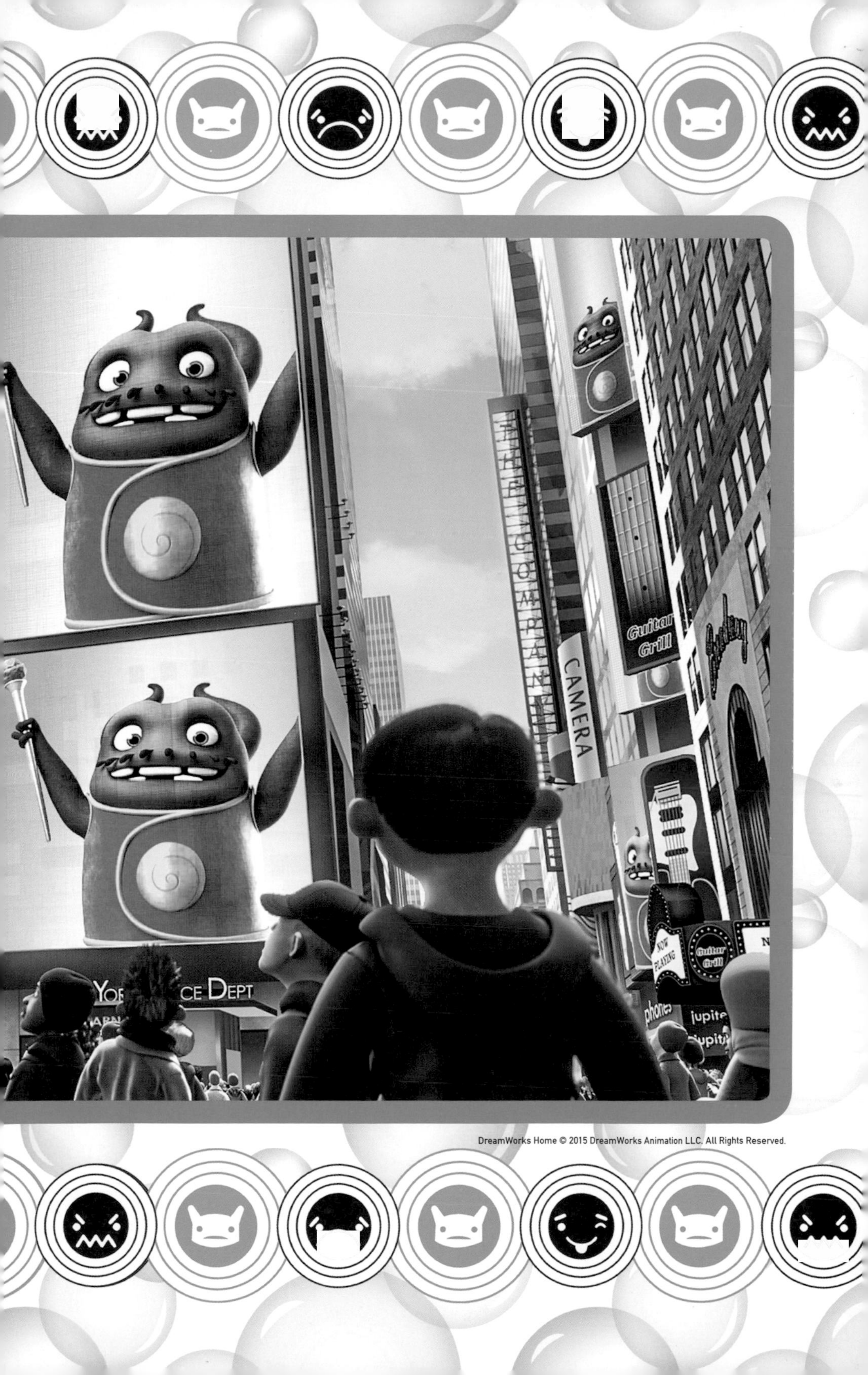
CAMERA
Guitar Grill
NOW PLAYING
Guitar Grill

PIG IN SPACE

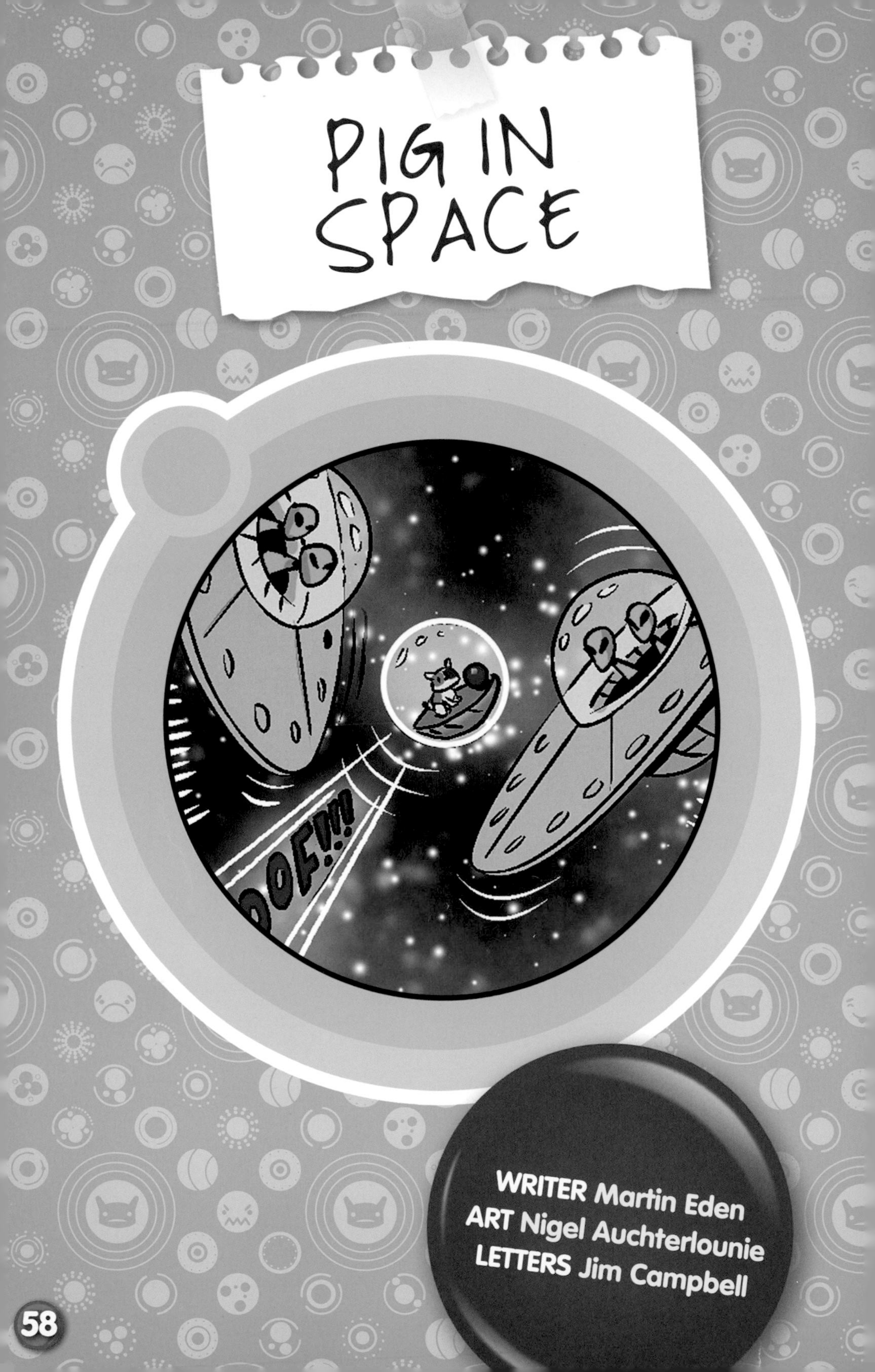

OOF!!!

WRITER Martin Eden
ART Nigel Auchterlounie
LETTERS Jim Campbell

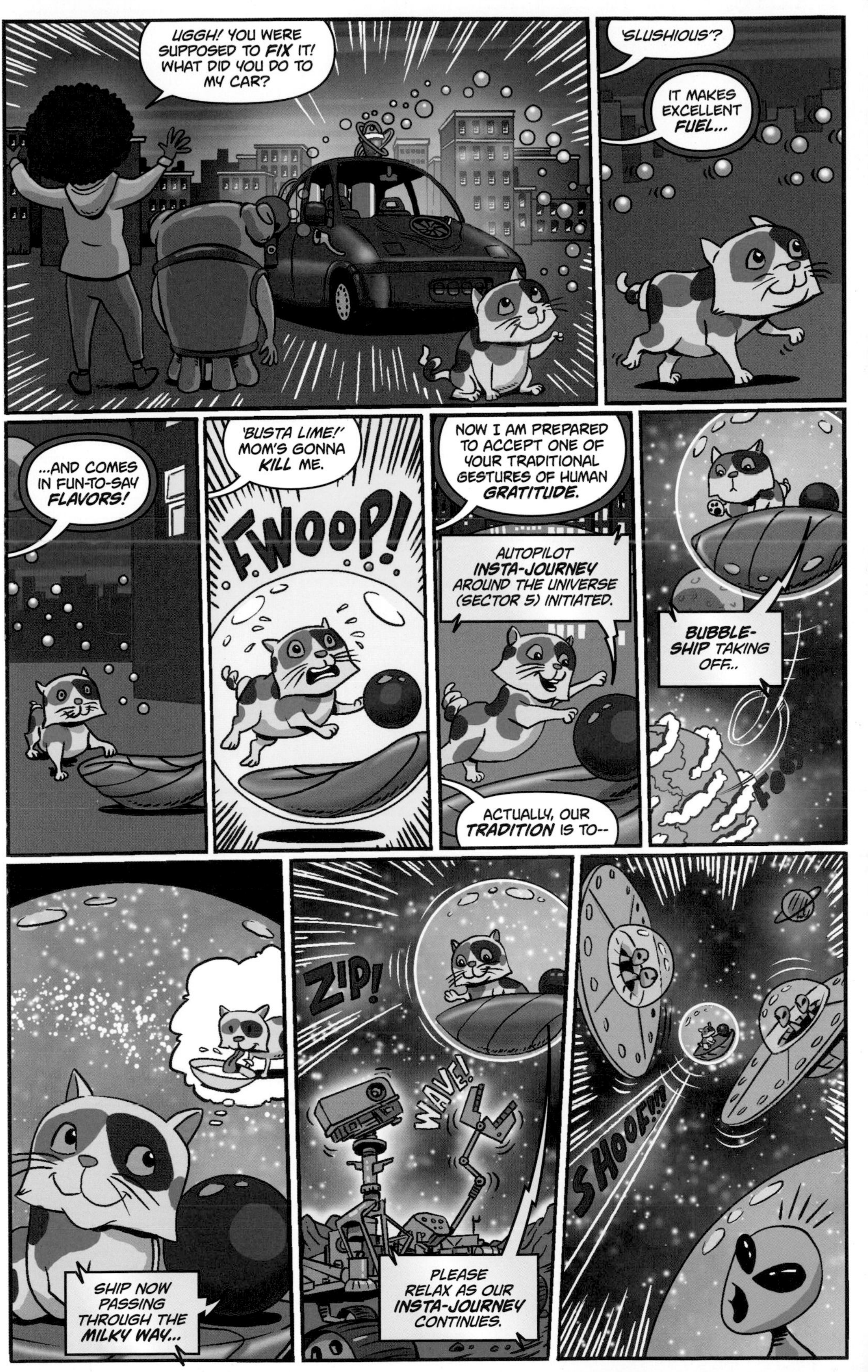
UGGH! YOU WERE SUPPOSED TO FIX IT! WHAT DID YOU DO TO MY CAR?
'SLUSHIOUS'?
IT MAKES EXCELLENT FUEL...
...AND COMES IN FUN-TO-SAY FLAVORS!
'BUSTA LIME!' MOM'S GONNA KILL ME.
FWOOP!
NOW I AM PREPARED TO ACCEPT ONE OF YOUR TRADITIONAL GESTURES OF HUMAN GRATITUDE.
AUTOPILOT INSTA-JOURNEY AROUND THE UNIVERSE (SECTOR 5) INITIATED.
ACTUALLY, OUR TRADITION IS TO--
BUBBLE-SHIP TAKING OFF...
SHIP NOW PASSING THROUGH THE MILKY WAY...
ZIP!
WAVE!
PLEASE RELAX AS OUR INSTA-JOURNEY CONTINUES.
SHOOF!!!

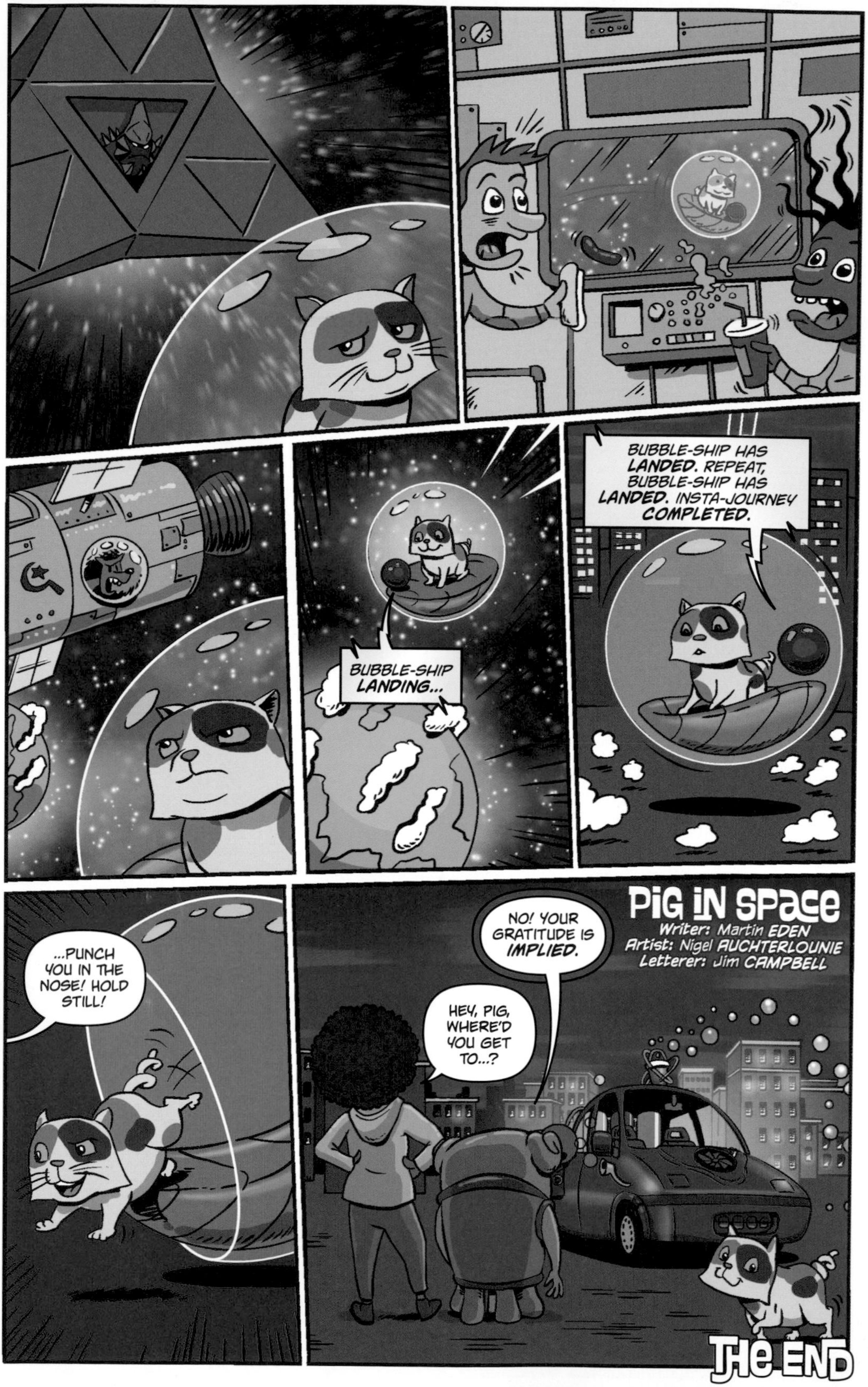
BUBBLE-SHIP LANDING...
BUBBLE-SHIP HAS LANDED. REPEAT, BUBBLE-SHIP HAS LANDED. INSTA-JOURNEY COMPLETED.
...PUNCH YOU IN THE NOSE! HOLD STILL!
PIG IN SPACE
Writer: Martin EDEN
Artist: Nigel AUCHTERLOUNIE
Letterer: Jim CAMPBELL
NO! YOUR GRATITUDE IS IMPLIED.
HEY, PIG, WHERE'D YOU GET TO...?
THE END

PENGUINS OF MADAGASCAR GRAPHIC NOVEL COLLECTION

DreamWorks
PENGUINS
of MADAGASCAR
OPERATION: HEIST

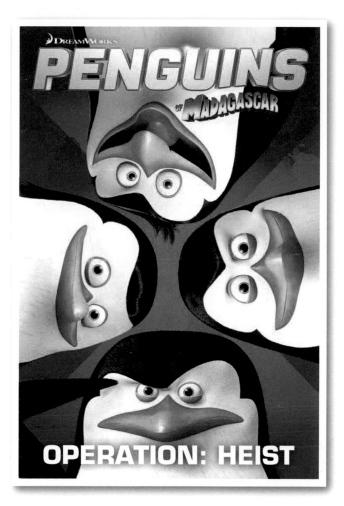

AWESOME COMIC STRIP ANTICS FROM THE *PENGUINS OF MADAGASCAR!*

You've seen them in their own brilliant movie, now read their hilarious comic strips in this brand new collection. In 'Big Top,' the penguins' circus gets a new recruit – the mysterious Claude the Clown... And then in 'Operation: Heist,' arch-villain Clepto the Magpie is on the loose, and he brainwashes Rico into doing his dirty work!

VOLUME 2 ON SALE NOW!

WWW.TITAN-COMICS.COM

TITAN COMICS

DREAMWORKS ANIMATION SKG

DREAMWORKS DRAGONS: RIDERS OF BERK

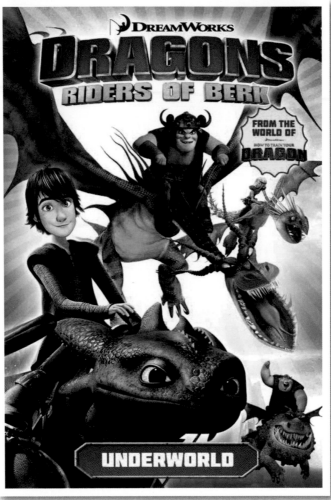

VOLUMES 1 TO 5 ALSO AVAILABLE ONLINE AND IN ALL GOOD BOOKSTORES!

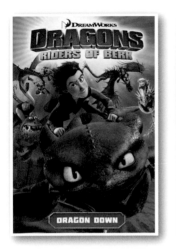

DreamWorks
DRAGONS
RIDERS OF BERK
DRAGON DOWN

VOLUME 1

DreamWorks
DRAGONS
RIDERS OF BERK
DANGERS OF THE DEEP

VOLUME 2

DreamWorks
DRAGONS
RIDERS OF BERK
THE ICE CASTLE

VOLUME 3

DreamWorks
DRAGONS
RIDERS OF BERK
THE STOWAWAY

VOLUME 4

DreamWorks
DRAGONS
RIDERS OF BERK
FROM THE WORLD OF
DRAGON
THE LEGEND OF RAGNAROK

VOLUME 5

WWW.TITAN-COMICS.COM

DreamWorks Animation SKG

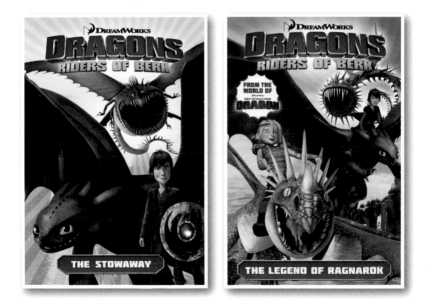

KUNG FU PANDA
GRAPHIC NOVEL COLLECTION

DREAMWORKS
KUNG FU PANDA
VOLUME 1
TITAN COMICS
Kung Fu Panda © 2015 DreamWorks Animation LLC. All Rights Reserved.

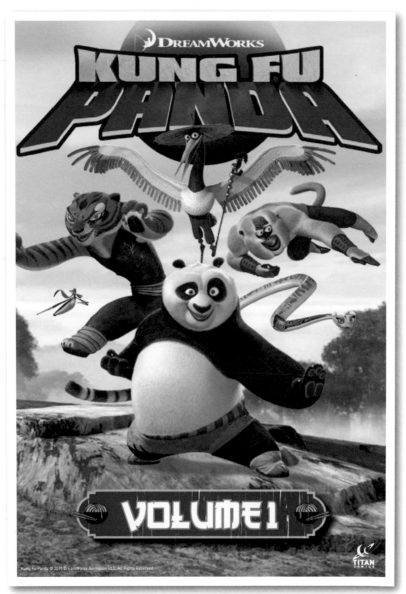

VOLUME 1 COMING SOON!
WWW.TITAN-COMICS.COM